CW01373328

Books by Megs Pritchard

Valentine's Surprise - Standalone Novella

Crossing Desires Series:

Awakening

Struggle

Terrible Twos - Standalone Novel

Second Chances Series:

Take a Chance

New Beginnings

Book Two

Second Chances series

By

Megs Pritchard

New Beginnings

Book Two in the Second Chances series

Copyright © 2017 Megs Pritchard

www.megspritchardauthor.com

Edited by Jessica McKenna - www.liteditor.com

Cover art © Jay Aheer of Simply Defined Art - www.simplydefinedart.com

All rights reserved. This book is licensed to the original purchaser only.

No part of this publication may be reproduced, distributed, or transmitted in any form or by any means, including photocopying, recording, or other electronic or mechanical methods. It is illegal and a violation of international copyright law, subject to prosecution and upon conviction, fines and/or imprisonment. Any eBook format cannot legally be loaned or given to others. For permission requests, write to the publisher.

This is a work of fiction. Names, characters, places, and incidents either are the product of the author's imagination or are used fictitiously, and any resemblances to the actual person, living or dead, business establishments, events, or locales is entirely coincidental.

WARNING

This book contains explicit M/M sexual scenes and strong language. It is intended for mature, adult audiences only.

Dedication

To Helen. Thank you for all the invaluable information you gave me when it came to solicitors.

To my amazing and slightly crazy boys. You drive me nuts, but I love you. Never change.

To my Dad, who was a little confused as to why I wanted to write about men but supported me throughout this journey.

Love you

Chapter One

Geoff Foster sat in his study, finishing the summary of an ongoing case. It still needed some more touches, but he was finally close to finishing the first draft of his closing argument and, as lead solicitor, it needed to be strong.

When Geoff finished, he dropped his pen down and stretched his arms over his head, groaning as the tension eased from his tight muscles. He loved being a solicitor but sometimes the job appeared to be all about the paperwork and less about the clients.

Standing, Geoff walked over to the window, placing a hand on the glass. The cold penetrated his skin, and he shivered at the difference in temperature. The study and his body were far warmer than outside. He sighed looking at the darkening sky. It seemed to be taking a long time for spring to arrive.

He turned, looking back at his desk, seeing the paperwork gathered on it. He was now part owner of his father's company, and he enjoyed the work but not the headaches that came with being the boss. He would rather be sat in court representing a client than dealing with the running of a business. He sighed walking back to his desk and sat down looking over the figures his accountant had sent him that morning.

When he heard a floorboard creak above him, he lifted his head and stared at the ceiling. Was Ben finally getting out of bed?

Geoff had only known Ben through Sebastian, an employee, due to his relationship with Tom. Seb and Tom had known each other as teenagers, but when Tom had been thrown out by his parents for being gay, they had lost touch.

Tom had spent four years on the street as a prostitute when Seb had seen him one night. Seb had pursued Tom, refusing to leave him to live that life, and during this time, they had fallen in love.

At the same time, a friend of Ben and Tom's, Adam, had been murdered. Ben, feeling guilty over his death, had attempted suicide. This, in turn, led Geoff to Ben when he'd helped Seb and Tom. And now Seb not only had Tom living with him but Matt and Luke, another two teenagers who had been living with Tom and Ben.

When Geoff had seen Tom's friend lying in that hospital bed, he knew he couldn't leave him there alone. Ben had been pale, thin, and the dark shadows under his eyes testified to the difficult life he'd been living. Geoff had made the decision to bring Ben back to his house when he was discharged from hospital so Geoff could aid him in his recovery after his failed suicide attempt.

The sound of the doorbell ringing dragged Geoff from his thoughts, and when he looked at the clock, he realised it was later than he'd thought. Getting up, Geoff took his glasses off and placed them on the desk before walking to the front door to answer it.

When he opened it, he found Seb and Tom stood there. "Hey, come in," he told them, holding the door open for them.

"We're not disturbing you, are we?" Seb asked as they walked in.

"No, not really. Just finishing my closing statement for the Peterson case and going over the figures," Geoff answered, closing the door behind them.

Seb was slightly taller than Tom, with black hair and hazel eyes. Tom had short blond hair, having recently cut it, and blue eyes. When Geoff had first met Tom, he'd been thin, but now he'd put weight on and looked much healthier for it. He'd lost the dark circles from under his eyes and had more colour in his cheeks, but Tom still appeared wary around Geoff.

"How's Ben been? Any better?" Tom asked as they walked through the house and into the kitchen.

Since Ben's release from the hospital, he'd isolated himself from everyone and remained in his bedroom. None of the others had been able to reach him, and it was causing some concern for Geoff. The last thing Geoff wanted was for Ben to attempt to end his life again. The isolation and apparent depression could cause Ben to do something he wouldn't under normal circumstances, or whatever normal had been for him while living on the streets.

"No change really. Ben still appears depressed, but, with him isolating himself to his bedroom, he hasn't had any real opportunity to attempt to harm himself again." After Adam's body had been found, Ben had felt responsible because he hadn't been there to watch his friend's back. It wasn't Ben's fault-- Adam had run off, and Ben hadn't been able to find him. Still, Ben appeared to feel like it was his fault that he had let his friend die and so had tried to kill himself.

"I know. It's been two months now, and I was hoping he would have started to come around. I wish I'd been there," Tom muttered.

"Hey, it wasn't your fault. We've talked about this, haven't we?"

Seb said to him, hugging him close.

"Seb's right. From what you've told me, it appears, for whatever reason, Adam was taking unnecessary chances with his life. Why else would he have gone out and not waited for anyone to be there for him? He was aware of how dangerous the streets were," Geoff added. He knew how hard Seb had worked to help Tom move past his own guilt over Adam's death.

"I know, course I fuckin' know. But he was my friend, and I feel like I let him down, that if I'd been there things might have been different. The attack a couple of weeks before seemed to be some trigger that made him change. He was never that fuckin' reckless, well, not that I'd noticed."

"Come on, Tom. We can't change what's happened, can we? For now, we need to be there for Ben." Seb tried to comfort Tom, but it appeared that Tom still wasn't fully over what had happened either.

"Tom, have you thought about talking to someone about what you've been through?" Geoff asked him. He knew Seb had tried to arrange for Tom to see a counsellor, but so far he'd had no luck. Tom refused to talk to anyone. Geoff believed all four of them needed to talk about their experiences living on the streets. To discuss everything they had been through, what they had witnessed, and having to sell sex to survive. Geoff wasn't certain if it was something he could have done if he was in a similar situation and he admired the strength they all seemed to possess. None of them had turned to drugs. Well, with the exception of Adam.

It had only come out after his death that Adam had been using, and this may have contributed to his behaviour. It had been a shock to Tom, Matt and Luke to find out about Adam's drug use. Ben hadn't been told yet, and Geoff wasn't sure if he was ready to hear about it. Ben didn't need to know about that. He'd probably blame himself for that too.

"Not this again." Tom closed his eye briefly, rubbing his head. "I don't want to see or talk to anyone. Fresh start right? So why go over all of it? It's done. It's over." Tom swiped a hand out in front of him, staring at Seb and Geoff.

"How about a journal? I've read that sometimes if a person doesn't want to talk about what has happened in their life then writing it down can help. You could write down your experiences, what you went through. It might help with some things," Seb said to Tom.

"What? Is it gang up on Tom time? Well, I can tell you what you can do--"

"Don't get angry, Tom," Geoff interrupted. "We're just concerned for you. What you've been through will have left some mark, and Seb wants to help you. I was the one who suggested it, so don't be angry with him. If you want to be angry at anyone, be angry at me. You don't have to go and see anyone, but just think about it, alright?" Geoff paused, taking a deep breath in. "Now, what do you want to drink?"

Both asked for coffees and Geoff started the coffee machine. He could hear them talking quietly behind him and he didn't want to interrupt. It was clear that Tom was angry over what had been said, but Geoff believed that speaking to someone would help him.

Geoff liked Tom, and he made Seb happy, which he needed with everything that was happening with his parents. They still had issues with him being in a relationship with Tom. They still phoned the office to try and obtain information about Seb, how he was doing at work and what was happening in his life.

Seb's parents never mentioned Tom by name, simply referred to him as 'that boy' or 'it.' Why they couldn't speak to Seb directly confused Geoff. He was their son, and they had refused to talk to him because of his relationship with Tom.

Geoff knew Tom's parents had thrown him out for being gay, but he didn't know Ben's story yet. Ben barely spoke, barely ate or slept. He could hear him moving around his room at night and worse were the times when he could hear him cry. He'd lost count of the number of times he'd wanted to go into Ben's room and comfort him, but he knew Ben wouldn't want that. He wasn't ready for that yet. Ben didn't know him. Geoff was Seb's boss who had given him a place to stay after Adam's murder and Ben's subsequent failed suicide attempt. Geoff quietly sighed, finished making the coffee and handed Tom and Seb a mug each.

"Do you want to go up and see him?" he asked Tom.

Tom nodded as he blew on his coffee. "Yeah, I will in a few minutes. I just need to warm up first. Can't believe how cold it is at the moment."

"Yes, it certainly is." Geoff paused, thinking of a way to ask Tom about Ben. He didn't want to upset him by asking personal questions, but he needed answers.

He cleared his throat. "Tom, do you know how Ben ended up on the streets? He hasn't talked much and if I'm going to be of any assistance to him, knowing some of his background would help."

Tom shook his head, pursing his lips. "No. We never really talked about stuff like that." Tom paused, frowning. "What we had wasn't that usual, I guess. I don't know many others who all lived together like we did, doing what we did." Tom shrugged. "But, I didn't hang out with many others. It was just a case of surviving really."

Geoff nodded, listening to Tom. Ben appeared to be a private individual, if he understood Tom correctly. Ben hadn't talked much, but the few words he'd spoken hadn't included anything about his family or friends. Geoff had asked some questions but realised quickly that Ben would clam up and then wouldn't talk at all. In fact, he barely looked him in the eye.

Being a solicitor helped. Geoff knew when to push and when to pull back. He knew how to ask the right questions in a non-threatening way. He would have to be patient and wait for Ben to trust him and then he would hopefully open up to him. All in good time.

"What was it like?"

Tom looked at him, and Geoff held his stare. He wanted to know what Ben had experienced. He watched as Tom clenched his jaw and his hand tightened on the mug he held.

"What do you think it was fuckin' like?" Tom snapped at him.

"You tell me, Tom. If I'm to be of any help to Ben, I need to know something of what you went through, how you lived."

Tom paused before speaking. "Sure, why not. It was a piece of piss. Easy--"

"Tom, don't be like this. Please," Seb spoke to him quietly.

"Look, I don't want an argument, but I do want to help Ben. Anything you can tell me will be kept between us." Geoff held his hand out palm upwards towards Tom.

"I don't want to talk about it. I don't want to have to go through all that shit again. It was fuckin' hard enough living it." Tom shook his head and sighed deeply. "Look, let me think about it, alright? I know you want to help him, just give me some time. It wasn't easy doing what we did. You had to learn to shut parts of yourself off when things happened to you, when you had to perform. That's why so many turn to drugs or get pissed. Living on the streets is fuckin' hard."

"Thanks. I appreciate it. I know I'm asking a lot of you, but I wouldn't have asked you if I didn't think it would help me in some way to understand where Ben is right now."

"Is he talking at all?" Tom asked him.

"Some, not much though. He's withdrawn and appears depressed. I have to force him to eat, otherwise he would starve. He rarely leaves his room and don't even ask me about his personal hygiene." Geoff shook his head.

"Sounds like depression," Seb commented after hearing Geoff's description of Ben.

Geoff nodded. "Yes. I'm fairly certain it is. That's why I want him to see a professional. He might need antidepressants, and I can't be here all the time to watch over him. I need to get back to the office and see everyone. If I thought it would help him, I'd have him come in and do some work. He seems intelligent, well, that's when we manage to have a conversation that lasts longer than five minutes."

"He is smart, very smart. I always wondered why he was on the streets, but he never talked about it. At all. None of us knows. Maybe he told Adam, but I guess we'll never know now." Tom put his mug down on the counter and turned to Seb. "I'm going up to see him."

Geoff watched Tom and Seb briefly kiss before Tom left the kitchen. When Geoff was certain Tom wouldn't hear them, Geoff smiled at Seb and asked, "How is everything between you two?"

Seb looked at him and shrugged. "As expected I guess. He has more good days than bad. Four years on the streets has to have taken its toll on him, you know. He has these trust issues." Seb gave Geoff a small smile. "I guess he's waiting for the other shoe to drop. I know he's waiting for me to realise I've made a mistake and kick him out. I can understand that, but I wish he could just believe me when I say that that isn't going to happen."

"It'll take time. As you said, he's been through a lot and you being there for him now is helping him, even if it doesn't appear that way. How are Matt and Luke?"

Seb chuckled. "Matt is turning out to be a bit of a prankster. He likes to get you unawares. They're both talking about going to college, and Matt has an interview at the shop near us. Luke seems to be taking longer to settle, but he's surprisingly shy, considering everything he's been through. Tom told me that they seem a lot better compared to when they lived in that house."

"You did a good thing with them, you know that, right? Not everyone would have opened their door and given them a place to live."

"I couldn't leave them there, not after everything that had happened and I know Tom wouldn't have left them. And you're helping too." Geoff nodded but didn't interrupt. "Maybe it's selfish. I wanted Tom to move in, and I knew he wouldn't leave them so..." Seb shrugged and stopped talking.

"Whatever the reasons were, you still did it. You know they both came to see Ben yesterday?"

"Yeah, they mentioned it. That's part of the reason Tom wanted to come over as well. He thinks if Ben sees people he knows it might help him."

Geoff nodded. "We can only try."

They both stood silent for a minute drinking their coffee before Seb spoke.

"So, are you working on anything?"

"The Peterson case and it's not easy going. I needed a break, so I'm glad you came. Let's go in the living room while we wait for Tom."

Geoff walked into the living room and sat on the sofa while Seb sat on the chair. He had gotten to know Seb a little better now they saw each other outside of work. He'd always liked him; he was a good worker and tried to help other people in the office. Geoff knew he'd made the right decision by giving him a permanent contract. The downside was the phone calls he was constantly receiving from Seb's parents. He hadn't told Seb he was receiving several a week. He knew Seb would be embarrassed about it and, at the end of the day, Seb had done nothing wrong. You loved who you loved. It was his parents who clearly had issues. Still, Geoff wondered about Seb's parents and what Seb knew.

"Have you heard from your parents?" Geoff asked him taking a sip of his coffee.

Seb snorted. "The usual. They won't have anything to do with me while Tom is on the scene. I wish they could get over it and just accept that Tom is in my life now. Apparently, I need to 're-evaluate my lifestyle choices', that's a direct quote by the way, and follow God's plan. Like God cares about who I love. We haven't spoken recently and it doesn't look like we will anytime soon."

"Have they always been like this?"

Seb frowned, leaning forward in the chair. "They always made the odd comment, but never to the extreme they do now. I told you that they turned their backs on Tom when his parents threw him out. I never thought they'd be capable of doing something like that. They'd known Tom for years. Tom was either at our house, or Josh was at his. They were so close." Seb shook his head. "To suddenly have everything taken away from you. Tom must have been so scared."

Geoff would never be able to understand how parents could treat their own children like that. To abandon them simply because of their sexual orientation. Yet, he knew it happened and more regularly than the papers reported. It was a crime that was never seen and he'd witnessed some of them during his thirty-two years. From the boy at school to one of the cases he'd taken on.

They talked some more about nothing important until they heard Tom walk through the door.

"How is he?" Geoff asked him, standing.

"He talked a little. Not much though. I just told him about everything that's happening. He doesn't seem as bad as he was, but it's only been a few weeks."

Seb stood up and walked over to him, putting his hand on the back of Tom's neck. "Want to go home?"

Tom nodded. Geoff noticed that his face was pale and his shoulders were slumped.

"Yeah. Thanks, Geoff, for everything."

Geoff stood up and also walked over to Tom. "You don't have to thank me. Come over whenever you want. He needs to see the people he knows."

Geoff walked to the door and watched Seb and Tom get into Seb's car before shutting the door. He locked up and walked back to the kitchen where he slowly looked up at the ceiling. What was Ben thinking right now? He had to be hurting. He just wished he would let him in to help. Sighing, Geoff made a fresh batch of coffee before going back into his study to resume working the Peterson case.

New Beginnings

Chapter Two

Ben Parker lay on his bed staring at the ceiling. He didn't want to get up. He didn't want to do anything. He wanted to lie there and let everything wash over him. Let life forget about him.

His body was heavy, his eyes ached and were puffy to the touch. His throat was scratchy and his chest tight. But, none of that mattered now. How he felt didn't matter now. He couldn't be bothered about anything, and didn't give a shit about his health. He'd lost his friends, and he knew it was his fault.

If only he had fought harder with Adam. If only he'd managed to catch up with him when he'd left the house that night, then none of this would have happened. What made it worse was where he was now living. A nice, warm house with food in the cupboards, a proper bed and hot, clean water. If Adam hadn't have died, they would still be on the streets. It felt like he had somehow gotten lucky because his friend was no longer alive.

He couldn't stop replaying the night Adam had left in his mind. It was the last time he'd seen Adam alive. He kept running through everything he'd said and then changing the words so that Adam had stayed. He kept questioning his actions, the way he spoke, the way he had shouted.

Rolling over onto his side, Ben curled up into a ball. His throat hurt, and he struggled to swallow. He closed his eyes as he clutched the covers to him and rubbed the sheet over his lips before pulling it away and biting his bottom lip hard. It was only when he tasted blood that he stopped. The pain seemed to distract him from his thoughts, but not for long.

Opening his eyes, Ben stared at the light green wallpaper, the same one he had been staring at for weeks now. He glanced around the room, once again taking the decor in. The floorboards had been sanded then varnished an oak colour. The furniture was made of pine, and the curtains and bedding matched the wallpaper. It was a nice room, a room he felt comfortable in, and again Ben was overwhelmed by the guilt that welled up inside of him. There he was enjoying his surroundings when Adam had nothing but a cold, dark room for company.

Part of him wished he had died instead; he deserved it for letting his friend down. He was a worthless piece of shit, and when it came down to it, he couldn't even end his own life. And he'd thought about it. A lot. Never had the guts to do it. He was such a chicken shit, pussy.

Maybe he deserved some good luck of his own after everything he'd experienced. Ben shook his head. What a stupid thought. Of course he didn't. Why was he even thinking like that? He deserved all the shit he'd endured. Probably even more. He was pathetic. Nothing more than a stain.

But, hadn't he suffered enough?

New Beginnings

Not according to what his step-dad used to say. That's why he was a worthless piece of shit and had nothing to offer anyone. Shit son, that's what his mum used to say to him. Didn't know why she fed him or kept a roof over his head. Wasting good money on him.

It was his fault his real dad had left. That was what Derek, his step-dad, always said. That was why he beat him. Had to try and beat some worth into him, make him a man, all while his mum would watch, encouraging him.

But, how could it have been his fault? He was just a child. It had to be his fault though, because that was what they'd told him.

Adam had paid the price. He'd died because of him, so maybe they'd had a point. Ben wasn't worth the air he breathed. Why hadn't he died instead?

Every time he closed his eyes he would see Adam. Adam smiling and laughing. Adam somehow enjoying himself, even with the life they had. He always tried to find the good in their situation. No one telling them what to do. No rules to obey. Free, Adam would say, to do what they wanted.

He'd met Adam at Canal Street one Saturday night. Both of them were working at the time. Adam hadn't liked the fact that Ben had approached him. Ben smiled slightly remembering how Adam had acted that night. He'd been a right prickly bastard. Didn't want to give Ben the time of day.

He could remember their first conversation like it had happened yesterday. He'd stood looking at Adam, dressed in his skinny jeans, tight shirt and trainers, watching how he handled potential punters. A little cocky, but he always seemed to get his man. Never gone for too long before he was back, then right back to business.

Even though he hated what he was doing, he couldn't help but admire the ease with which Adam worked. It wasn't until much later when they'd gotten to know each other that he'd confided in him. It took a lot of mental preparation for him to get into the right mindset to do the job.

Ben had approached Adam to talk to him and had managed a muttered, 'Hi.' Adam had turned and stared at him, looking him up and down before he'd turned away, dismissing him.

"What the fuck do you want?" he'd said with a scowl on his face and continued looking for work.

That had made Ben pause. He hadn't been sure if he should continue. "I just wanted to say hi."

"Well you've said it, so fuck off."

Ben had been startled by the way Adam had spoken to him. At the time, he'd thought he'd made a mistake coming over to speak to him. Nodding his head, he'd turned to walk away, mumbling, "Okay, sorry man."

"How long?"

Ben had turned back to Adam. "What?"

Adam had sighed before asking again. "Doing this. How long?"

"Not long. Why?"

"It shows."

"What do you mean, 'it shows?'" Ben scowled at Adam.

Adam had waved a hand in his direction. "The way you act, the way you stand. Everything shows you're new at this. Unless it's an act. Is it? Does it work? How many a night?"

"Look, I've only been doing this a couple of months, so I guess it shows. I have no idea what I'm doing here." Ben swallowed. "I'm just trying to survive. I need help."

Adam had slowly looked him up and down again. "Yep, you definitely need help."

"Will you?"

"Will I what?" Adam had asked while smiling smugly at him.

"Will you help me?"

"I'll think about it." With that, Adam had turned and walked away from him, leaving him standing there staring at him.

The next time Ben had seen Adam, he'd taken him to a small cafe, explained everything to him, and that had been the start of their friendship.

A knock on the bedroom door brought him out of the past and back into the present. He frowned, tensing as he stared at the opening door. He watched Geoff walk into the room and smile slightly at him.

"I'm about to cook some dinner. Nothing much, just a stew. Would you like some?"

"No," Ben answered as he shook his head.

Geoff frowned at him before commenting, "You've not eaten today, and I know you didn't each much yesterday either. You need to have something."

"I'm not hungry."

Geoff walked closer, squatting by the side of the bed. "You need to eat, Ben. This isn't good for you."

"I said, I wasn't hungry," Ben told him through gritted teeth, narrowing his eyes at Geoff.

Geoff sighed. "Please eat something. You're going--"

"I said no! Now fuck off!" Ben screamed at him. Why couldn't the guy just leave him the fuck alone! He watched Geoff's face harden as he stood. Geoff nodded and then left the room, closing the door quietly behind him. As soon as the door closed, the tension left Ben's muscles and he sighed.

The guy just couldn't take a hint! Yeah, he should be grateful that he was letting him stay in his house, but he just didn't give a shit about that, well, about anything actually. He just wanted to lie there and be left alone to do nothing. He had no appetite, no desire to get up, and no desire to do anything.

Maybe part of him wanted to get kicked out. It would make things easier for him. On the streets, he could disappear and never be seen again. On the streets, it wouldn't take too long for something to happen to him, something he deserved. Then he wouldn't have to end his own life. The choice would be taken from him. He clearly couldn't do it himself. The one time he'd worked up the guts to do it, he'd failed. He was that useless he couldn't even kill himself.

He heard the knock on the door but didn't turn towards it when it opened. He was aware of Geoff walking over to him and putting something on the bedside cabinet next to him. He ignored him when he stood there looking at him. He heard Geoff sigh and then leave the room, closing the door behind him. He turned to see what Geoff had left, finding a sandwich and what looked like some juice in a glass.

He rolled over away from the food and faced the bedroom wall. He didn't want the food, hadn't he told him that? Why did he keep on doing this? He just wanted to be left alone, left to lie there and not do anything. He didn't want to do anything. He didn't want to live. Why couldn't anyone understand that? Tom, Matt and Luke kept coming to see him. Kept trying to draw him out and make him be a part of things. They were out of that world and looked like they might have a chance at a normal life, but that wasn't for him. He had nothing to give, nothing to offer.

He was worthless. Why couldn't anyone see that?

New Beginnings

※ ※ ※

Geoff walked downstairs, leaving the food, and knew Ben wouldn't eat any of it. He'd been trying to get him to eat and come out of his room, but nothing seemed to be working. It looked like it was time for some form of intervention. Ben needed to see a doctor or psychiatrist. Geoff knew Ben had issues, and he didn't think they were all related to what he had been doing on the streets either. Tom, Matt and Luke had all lived that same life, and they appeared to be adjusting well now. He knew that Ben might be suffering from depression; his friend had been murdered, and he hadn't been there to help him.

Walking into his study, Geoff dropped heavily into the chair, staring out of the window. He rested his chin on his hand, thinking about his next course of action. What did he do? Did he leave Ben and see if his behaviour changed? Or did he intervene? How would Ben react if he did intervene?

Making his decision, Geoff picked up his contacts list and thumbed through until he found the number he wanted. Dr Clara Rimmer. He'd worked on a case with her a couple of years back. One of the first important cases he'd taken on. During the case, they'd become good friends and had kept in touch. Geoff knew if anyone could help, it would be Clara.

Checking the time to make sure it wasn't too late, Geoff dialled her number and waited for her to answer. After a couple of rings, he heard her voice.

"Hello, Dr Rimmer speaking."

"Hi Clara. It's me, Geoff."

"Hi, how're you doing?" she answered warmly.

"I'm good, thanks. How's the family doing?"

"We're all good. Thanks for asking. Now, why don't you tell me why you called?"

"What? I need a reason to call now?" Geoff laughed.

"Never, but knowing you, you would normally still be in the office working, not calling me," Clara told him.

"You're good. I'll give you that." Geoff laughed again. Damn, Clara was good. "Yeah, you're right, I do need some advice."

"Alright. Tell me what's happening, and I'll see what I can do."

Geoff spent the next few minutes explaining the situation to Clara, who asked a couple of questions but mainly remained quiet. When he'd finished, he sat in silence waiting for Clara to respond.

"So this behaviour he's displaying now has only started since the murder?"

"Yes. The attempted suicide happened after that."

"When he was released from the hospital, were any appointments set up for him?"

Geoff sighed. "Yes. He refused to go to any. I'm at a loss now as to how to help him. I've suggested seeing a counsellor, but he refused. To be honest, I'm struggling to get Ben to meet his most basic needs."

"Do you know why he ended up on the streets?" Good question.

"No, and I've spoken to the other three he lived with, and they didn't know either. It appears he didn't speak about it. It's frustrating. He appears to be fighting me every step of the way." Geoff sighed again, running a hand through his hair and slumping back in his chair.

Clara was silent again, and Geoff assumed she was thinking over what he'd told her. "Are you aware of the five stages of loss and grief?" She finally asked.

Geoff frowned. Five stages? "No, I've never heard of it. What is it

New Beginnings

and do you think Ben might be going through it?"

"There are five stages. First, there is denial and isolation, then anger followed by bargaining, depression and acceptance. You said Ben has isolated himself in his room. I wouldn't be surprised if he isn't going through scenarios in his mind and thinking of different outcomes if he had behaved differently. I wouldn't be surprised if he starts to display some anger at you. Shouting and throwing things. Have you seen any new marks or scratches on him?" Clara asked him.

"Not that I'm aware of, but I don't think he's showered much recently, so I can't answer that for you."

"Alright, I finish work early tomorrow, so I'll come and see Ben then. I'm not anticipating anything happening from this meeting, but at least I'll be able to see him and observe his behaviours."

Geoff sighed in relief rubbing his face. It felt as if a giant weight had been lifted off of him. "Thank you, Clara. You have no idea how grateful I am to you for coming."

"You might be, but I don't think Ben will be."

They talked for a few more minutes, catching up on events in each other's lives before they said their goodbyes. Geoff leaned back in his chair and stretched his arms above his head twisting his neck from side to side, releasing some of the tension gathered there.

Dropping his arms, Geoff sighed. He knew Ben was going to be furious with him for what he'd arranged, but it was for his benefit. Ben needed help, and Geoff hoped that this would be a step in the right direction. Part of him wondered if Ben would leave when he became aware of what was happening. He hoped not. The streets were certainly a place Ben shouldn't be anywhere near given his current frame of mind. He'd suffered enough.

What Geoff couldn't understand was why Ben would want to continue to suffer when it wasn't his fault. Maybe Clara was right, and this was part of the loss and grieving process he needed to work through. Whatever it was, Geoff would do the best he could to help Ben through it.

Chapter Three

Geoff knocked on the bedroom door the next morning. There was no response from inside the room. Trying again, Geoff knocked and waited. Again there was nothing. Sighing, Geoff opened the door and slowly entered the room.

A quick glance was enough for Geoff to see that Ben wasn't in the room. Frowning, he walked out of the bedroom and quickly checked the other rooms upstairs. When they all came up empty, Geoff called Ben's name, but there was no answer.

Walking back downstairs, Geoff searched the rooms until he found Ben sat in the living room, staring out of the window. Ben didn't acknowledge Geoff's presence or that he'd heard him calling his name. He remained sat in the chair, oblivious.

Geoff stood looking Ben over. It was clear he hadn't showered. His hair was greasy, overgrown and unkempt. The clothes he wore, he'd been wearing for several days now and were stained and wrinkled. As he approached him, Geoff could smell the stale, sweaty body odour pouring off of him and he grimaced. He couldn't allow this to continue.

Standing next to Ben, Geoff waited for him to acknowledge his presence, but after a couple of minutes, Geoff realised that wasn't going to happen. He'd planned on going into work today, but staring down at Ben, he wasn't sure whether he should do or if he should stay at home instead. He could have some files sent over, and he would be able to access any other information he needed from his computer at home. It wasn't the same as physically being in work, being able to interact with staff, see their facial expressions and body language, but it would have to do.

Geoff knew he couldn't keep Ben locked up, and he wanted him to come out of the bedroom and explore the house. But, a part of him was concerned as to what he would do when he was on his own. Would he try to hurt himself? Find a knife or pills and kill himself? Geoff couldn't allow that to happen. He had to try to reach Ben somehow.

Squatting in front of Ben, Geoff smiled. "Good morning, Ben. Did you sleep well?" He asked.

Ben didn't respond. In fact, he didn't even turn to look at him. Geoff waited, patiently, hoping the silence would cause Ben speak. After a minute of uncomfortable silence, Geoff tried again.

"I'm thinking of going into work today. Do you want me to pick anything up for you?"

Again there was no response.

"Ben. I'm speaking to you. Please answer me," Geoff spoke assertively.

Ben finally turned and looked at him, but Geoff could see the disinterest in his eyes by the blank expression on his face. "I'm fine," he whispered.

New Beginnings

Geoff nodded at him. Alright, he would go to the office until lunchtime and then come back. He would have to wait and see what had occurred in his absence. "Eat what you want. I'll be back later."

Geoff stood up and left the room. Grabbing a pen and a piece of paper, he wrote his contact details down. Walking back into the living room, he left them on the table next to where Ben sat.

"Here are my numbers if you need to speak to me. I won't be too long."

Waiting to see if Ben would acknowledge what he'd said, Geoff looked down at him, but all Ben did was turn away and stare out the window again, dismissing him. Geoff pursed his lips, staring at Ben before quietly sighing. Turning away, Geoff walked out of the room.

Grabbing his briefcase and a stack of files on his way, Geoff walked out of the house, closing the door gently behind in. He paused on the step and looked back at the shut door, contemplating his decision. Should he leave Ben?

Tightening his grip on the files, Geoff turned back to the door ready to open it and go back in but stopped. He'd only be gone a few hours. Enough time to see how Ben would behave. To see what Ben would do.

But, should he stay at home for another day and see how Ben was tomorrow? Would he be any better tomorrow? Geoff sighed and looked back at his car, squinting in the bright sunlight, the glare stabbing painfully into his eyes. He shivered slightly as the cold penetrated his clothes. Could he afford to stay at home another day? He had a business to run, and he'd neglected it recently, something he couldn't keep doing. Deciding he'd made the right choice, he walked over to his car and got in.

※ ※ ※

Ben turned to look at the doorway when he heard the front door close. He glanced around the living room taking in the decor and furniture. This was the first time he'd left his bedroom and had come downstairs. He took in the dark brown leather three seater sofa and a two seater sofa, the small table next to each and the tall lamps in the corners of the room.

The walls were painted in a light cream colour. The carpet was a similar colour to the sofa but was lush and thick under his bare feet. He rubbed his feet on the carpet, enjoying the feel of it as he sank them in. The focus of the room was the open fire, wood in the grate ready to be lit on a cold night.

Family pictures covered the wall in no particular pattern. The frames were all different shapes, sizes and colours, but seemed to fit together. In front of the open fire was a thick white rug; the type you could lie on with that special someone. Ben snorted to himself. Wasn't like he was going to have a special someone anytime soon, was it?

Standing up, he walked into the kitchen, another room he hadn't spent any time in. This room was all modern. He couldn't see any appliances so assumed they were all built into the units. The counter was black and marble, the units looked oak or maple, he wasn't sure. The island was designed using the same style and colours. He could see that there were drawers in half of it. The other half was a table and had bar stools around it. Being nosey, he pulled a few out, but they only contained the usual kitchen items.

In the corner, Ben saw that there were a table and chairs that didn't appear to match the kitchen. The table had a glass top, and there was a plastic mat rolled on top of it. One of the chairs had a booster seat attached. Ben frowned. Did Geoff have a child? He hadn't heard one in the house.

Lights hung down from the ceiling, and when he looked for the cooker, he found it was one of the touch types that lay flat on the surface. Running a hand along the counter, he could feel the cold and smoothness of the marble. A lot of money had been spent in this kitchen.

It was very different to the one in the house where he had lived. He couldn't call it a home, not after Derek had moved in. The only reason the house was clean or there was food on the table was because of him. He had to earn his place or he would have been punished, and that was something Ben never wanted to endure again.

Opening up cupboards, he eventually found the glasses, and again searching, he found the fridge and poured himself a glass of orange juice. He sat on one of the chairs by the island and drank it slowly.

Looking around the immaculate kitchen, he felt out of place. He didn't belong here. He didn't belong anywhere. Why wasn't he dead? God, he was such a fuck up! He couldn't even kill himself. Why did Tom and Seb have to find him?

Squeezing the glass, he suddenly stood up and threw it at the wall, screaming, watching it smash to pieces. Panting, Ben looked at the broken glass on the floor and sank to his knees. He was like the glass.

Broken.

※ ※ ※

Geoff put the phone down with a groan. After the call he'd just taken, he wished he'd stayed at home after all. Why was it that some people had more money than sense, and they thought they could buy themselves out of any trouble? So not only was he now representing someone who had been caught driving drunk, he now had to deal with the possibility that his client had attempted to bribe a police officer. Geoff knew he shouldn't have taken this case, but the client's father was a close friend of his own, so he'd felt an obligation to help. He should have refused. He knew the trouble that handling this case could bring.

He rubbed his forehead where he felt a headache developing, a painful pulsing sensation over his eyes. He closed them, breathing deeply, hoping to alleviate the pain.

When Geoff heard a knock on the door, he opened his eyes looking up to see Seb stood there. "Hey, come in." He sighed more than spoke the words.

Seb walked in and sat down in front of him. "Bad call?"

"Thomas Jefferson."

"Ah, enough said," Seb said with a grimace. "What's he done now?"

"Trying to bribe the arresting officer."

"What? And we're just hearing about this now?" Seb looked stunned, his eyes going wide as he shook his head. "Idiot."

"Yeah, I know. I wish I hadn't agreed to represent him." Geoff sighed, briefly closing his eyes, his headache worsening.

"Not like you had much choice."

"No, not really. Anyway, what can I help you with?" Geoff leaned forward and rested his arms on the desk in front of him, blinking as his eyes blurred. Shit, he was getting a migraine.

"It's about Ben. Tom's worried about him." Seb mimicked the action, leaning on Geoff's desk.

"Yeah, me too. A friend of mine is coming over tonight to speak to him."

"Ben agreed?" Seb sat back, eyebrows rising in surprise.

Geoff grimaced. "No. He doesn't know about it, but I feel he needs it. He's barely eating, doesn't leave the bedroom, and he doesn't talk. I can't get him to say anything to me. He's barely living. I don't even think he's had a shower."

"That bad?" Seb shook his head. "God."

"I know. Clara, she's the doctor I spoke to, suggested that he has a journal, so he can write down his thoughts and emotions. The same as you suggested with Tom." Geoff sat back, closing his eyes against the light flooding the room. It stabbed at his eyes, adding to the pain. "I don't know his past, so I don't know how to help him. I don't want to say anything that will inadvertently cause more harm. I'm going to buy a journal when I go for lunch, then I'll be heading back home. To be honest with you, I'm concerned about leaving him on his own for too long. I'm concerned as to what I'll be going back to."

"Does he seem suicidal to you?" Seb asked biting his lip.

"I don't know him well enough to say one way or the other. If I were to compare him to how he was when he left the hospital, then I would say no. He's had plenty of opportunities to do something and he hasn't. It's almost like he's given up, and he's waiting for the end. I'm hoping Clara will be able to tell me more after she's seen him. At least then, I'll be in a better position to help him."

"I only know Ben through what Tom, Matt and Luke have said. The person you're describing doesn't seem the same one they've told me about."

"I don't think it's about what he was doing. I think it goes deeper than that. We both know Tom was kicked out and had to fend for himself, but he doesn't seem to have been so deeply affected by what happened to Adam as Ben has. I think there's more to it, but again I can't say for certain because I know so little about him."

"It's frustrating, and I wish we could help more, but on a more positive note, both Matt and Luke have adjusted well."

"I'm glad. They're both great guys." Geoff meant what he said. All four had suffered enough. If only Ben could move forward.

Seb nodded, smiling. "I know it's not easy with all of us living together as we are but I'm glad I did it, and I know Tom is too. Anyway, when are you going to lunch?"

Geoff looked at the clock, noting the time. "In about an hour after I've sorted out this new mess in the Jefferson case." He grimaced, rubbing the bridge of his nose. "Not that I'm looking forward to it."

"Well, I'm glad it's yours and not mine. You have far more patience than I have when dealing with him."

Geoff grunted noncommittally. "Go now before I change my mind and pass this over to you."

Seb laughed, standing up. "No, thanks. I'm probably more likely to punch the bloke then help him."

Geoff spent the next hour making various phone calls and updating the case file with the relevant details. This case was going to be anything but easy. He wished he hadn't agreed to take it on but did he have a choice? He would have had his dad on his back if he hadn't had agreed. He was thirty-two and had all but taken over the company now his dad had dropped the number of cases and hours he worked. But, he still felt like he couldn't come into his own and make the company work the way he wanted it too. If it were his choice, he wouldn't take on these types of cases. Trying to get rich kids off-- rich kids who felt because they had money they were above the law-- drained him.

He sat back in his chair and closed his eyes, taking a deep breath in. He shook out his hands when he realised he held them clenched. Sighing again, he opened his eyes and sat forward in his chair, rubbing his forehead, and looked at his clock. It was time to leave.

He shut his computer off and grabbed the files he needed and walked out of his office, stopping to speak to Sue, his secretary, to update her. He managed to get away without being stopped and quickly left the building. Walking to his car, he opened it and left his files and briefcase before locking it and walking into the city centre. He went to the nearest bookshop and found what he wanted, purchased it and left, walking back to his car.

He wasn't flashy and his car reflected that. He didn't feel the need to spend stupid amounts of money on something that simply got him where he needed to go. Plus he babysat his brother's children, and with that in mind, he had a silver Citroen Grand C4 Picasso with a leather interior that was easier to clean. Getting in, he started the car and drove home.

Unlocking the door, Geoff walked into the hallway and paused as he listened to the house. Hearing nothing, he picked up the mail, quickly scanning through it. All junk. In the kitchen, he threw the mail in the bin before noticing the broken glass on the floor and stopped in his tracks. What had happened?

Frowning, Geoff quickly scanned the rest of the kitchen for any further signs of disturbances. When he saw none, he checked the rooms looking for Ben. Not finding him, he looked around for Ben and not seeing him anywhere he went upstairs and knocked on his bedroom door, opening it at the same time. Sticking his head in, he found Ben lying on the bed.

"Hi, Ben. How have you been today?"

Ben looked at him and shrugged his shoulders. Well, that was better than nothing. At least he acknowledged the question.

"I bought you something. It's a journal. I know you don't want to talk about what you've been through, so I thought it might help if you wrote it down instead. No one will see what you write unless you want them to. It doesn't just have to be about Adam, or your time on the streets, it can be about anything you want."

Goff walked over and placed the book and a pen on the cabinet next to the bed. He looked Ben over and noticed that he still hadn't showered or changed into clean clothes. The room was starting to smell, and Geoff was certain the bedding needed to be changed. But how did he approach that without upsetting Ben? He was glad he'd phoned Clara now. She would give him the insight he needed to help Ben or point him in the right direction.

"I'm going to make some lunch. Maybe some soup and a sandwich. What do you think?"

Ben shook his head but didn't look over at him.

"Well, I'll bring some up for you and if you decide you want it, it's there for you."

Geoff walked out of the room and closed the door before leaning back against it and closing his eyes. At least he'd gotten some response from him rather than being ignored or the blank stares. He cleaned up the broken glass and threw it out. What could have caused Ben to throw the glass?

In the kitchen, he gathered what he needed to make the sandwiches before putting some soup on to warm up. Leaning against the counter, Geoff stared at the tiles on the wall, pinching his lips together and frowning. He sighed, pushing away from the counter and running his hand through his hair. He started to pace the kitchen floor waiting for the food to warm. What should he do?

Stopping, Geoff looked down at the floor and crossed his arms over his chest. He knew he had to be patient. He knew he had to be understanding, but it was hard. He didn't have the correct tools to help Ben and he felt he was failing him. It was time he started reading about the five stages Clara had mentioned.

New Beginnings

Chapter Four

Ben rolled over, frowning at the sight of the journal. Why the fuck would he want to write about any of the shit that had happened in his life? Where had Geoff gotten that fucked up idea from? How could writing about his experiences help him? Ben felt his eyes start to itch and tingle and he squeezed them shut in an attempt to stop the tears from falling. He wouldn't cry! He didn't deserve his tears.

He was a worthless fuck up. He knew it. His parents had known it. Why write about it? He turned away from the journal, unable to look at.

After a few seconds, Ben glanced over at the journal again, staring at it. Should he write about it? About his experiences, about his parents and what they had done to him? He'd been thinking about them a lot recently. Not surprising, considering everything he'd been through. His step-dad and bitch of a mother.

The beatings, frequently being left without food and being forced naked into a dark cupboard and left for hours. He was still afraid of the dark. He could still remember sitting in that cupboard with his arms wrapped around his skinny legs trying to keep warm. Shivering, naked and afraid, he'd learned early on not to cry out. Starving, because they hadn't fed him again. Told he wasn't worth feeding and that he was a piss poor excuse for a son. Wasn't that why his real dad had abandoned them? He didn't want to accept that his son was a worthless piece of shit.

He still had the scars on his back from one of the beatings that he should have gone to the hospital for but they'd been too afraid to take him. How would they have been able to answer the questions regarding how the injuries had occurred? Broken bones were easier to explain. Overworked social workers were only too happy to have a plausible reason as to how his arm or leg had been broken. Falling off his bike or skateboard always sounded reasonable. The cigarette burns on his hips and thighs were never seen by professionals. Couldn't explain them away.

He tried to breathe, forcing the air into his lungs against the heaviness in his chest. The room started to blur and he closed his eyes. He heard the knock on the door and blinked his eyes rapidly. He didn't want Geoff to see him like this. The door opened and he looked over to see Geoff place a bowl and a sandwich next to the journal on the bedside cabinet.

"Chicken soup and a cheese sandwich. Come on, eat some of it. I'm not leaving until you do." Geoff stood close to the bed, arms crossed over his chest, watching Ben.

Ben watched Geoff, as Geoff waited for him to eat. Why couldn't he see that he wanted to be left alone? He didn't want to eat anything. It was all too much effort to move over to the food and eat it. His limbs were like lead and he didn't have the strength to move them. Tired. He was tired.

New Beginnings

Realising Geoff wasn't going anywhere soon, Ben mustered all the strength he could and sat up, stomach churning as he looked at the food. He reaching over to pick up the sandwich and took a bite. It tasted like sawdust to him, tacky and clumpy in his mouth. He found it difficult to chew because he had no saliva.

"Try some of the soup if you're struggling with the sandwich."

Geoff must have seen his difficulty. He dropped the sandwich back on the plate and tried some of the soup. After forcing himself to have several spoonfuls, he put it down. "I can't eat anymore."

"Come on, just a little bit more. Try finishing that half of the sandwich or a few more spoonfuls of soup."

"No, I can't."

"Please, just a bit more." Geoff held out the spoon with some soup on it. "I don't want to have to force feed you, but if you don't eat some more, you're going to make yourself ill."

Ben had a few more spoonfuls of soup before pushing it away. "I can't eat anymore, seriously."

"You're doing really well."

Ben shook his head. "No more."

"Please, just a-- "

"I said no!" Ben suddenly lunged forward and knocked the bowl from Geoff's hand, spilling the soup on him. Geoff jumped up when the hot soup touched him.

"Shit!"

Ben lay back down on the bed, watching Geoff compose himself before picking up the bowl and spoon and leaving the room. A couple of minutes later he returned, in clean jeans, and proceeded to clean the floor. Ben watched him, but didn't say a word.

Geoff stood and looked at him before turning and leaving the room. Ben exhaled the breath he'd been holding before closing his eyes and rolling over to face the wall. He wrapped his arms around his chest and lowered his head as he dug his nails into his arms until it hurt.

Pain. The pain helped. He needed it.

※ ※ ※

Geoff was in his study working when he heard the doorbell ring. Looking at the clock, he realised he'd spent the afternoon lost in his work and that Clara was probably here now. Walking to the front door, he opened it, smiling when he saw Clara. Standing to one side, Geoff opened the door wide and let her in. "Hi, Clara. Thanks for coming. Here let me take your coat."

He hung up her coat and then guided her to the kitchen. "Drink?"

"Coffee please."

He liked Clara, had from the first moment he'd met her. Tall and slim, with hair so blonde it was almost white and deep green eyes. Clara didn't bullshit you and that was what he respected about her.

Taking a mug from the cupboard, he poured some coffee into it and handed to her.

"How's Ben been?" she asked him as she blew on the hot liquid.

Geoff gave her a small smile. "I managed to get him to eat something."

"That's good. Some progress then."

"Don't know about that. When I pushed him to have more food, he knocked the bowl out of my hand." Geoff shrugged, leaning back against the counter.

Clara frowned for a few seconds then nodded as she blew on her coffee. "You can't push him, but you know that. Small steps, only when he feels comfortable. You need to go at his pace. Whether you believe it or not, Ben eating is a step in the right direction." Clara paused. "There is an element of trust there, whether he recognises it or not."

"I know." Geoff turned as he took a sip of his coffee. "I know I shouldn't have forced him to eat more." He shrugged. "But he was finally eating something and he hasn't been eating properly since he came here and I just wanted him to eat a little more."

"He's been through a lot from what you've told me. Whatever he went through at home that led him to a life on the streets, what he did to survive that. The murder of his friend, his suicide attempt and now his move here.

"Ben is a young man and he's experienced a lot of trauma in his life. Even someone older and more mature than him would have some difficulty adapting to all these changes and processing all the events in his life." Clara reached forward, placing her hand on Geoff's arm. "You know you're helping, even if it feels like you're not." Clara smiled at him as she spoke.

"Yeah, but it's frustrating! It seems like I'm sitting here, watching him slowly disappear and I don't know what to do to help." He paused before adding, "I looked up the five stages you mentioned. It was an interesting read and I can see some of the behaviours Ben is displaying matching the stages."

Clara nodded as she stared of into the distance. "Let me go up and speak with him."

"He might not say anything."

"That's fine. I can gather a lot about a person from their body language, more than you realise. Which room is he in?"

Geoff showed Clara to Ben's room and then left her alone. He came back down to his study and tried to go back to work, but found it impossible to do so. All he could think about was what might be going on upstairs.

Leaning back in his chair, Geoff thought back to the first time he'd seen Ben. It had been at the hospital. He'd gotten there before the ambulance and had seen Tom exit it, which was how he'd known which one Ben had been in.

He'd looked down at Ben as he had lain there, surprised at the feelings that seeing him had provoked in him. He'd seemed so small lying on the trolley, eyes closed, breathing mask on, and wires seeming to come from everywhere. He had wanted to hold him close and fight all his battles for him. To keep him safe from the darkness that seemed to be all around him. He'd been stunned at the emotions he'd felt. But the other thing he also remembered was how attractive he'd found him.

His lips twisted in a wry smile. Ben had been lying there trying to survive a suspected suicide attempt and Geoff had been thinking how attractive he was. He still did. Attractive and wounded and lost. He had brown hair with the most amazing eyes. A blue green that changed colour depending on how the light reflected off them.

Getting up from the chair, Geoff walked over to the window and looked out over his garden. He pushed his hands into his pockets and leaned against the wall next to the window, smiling when he saw a couple of robins enjoying the water bath in his garden. Spring was in the air and the trees and bushes were starting to bud again. Everything felt fresh and new.

Geoff knew he was lucky. The firm his father had established was doing well and it was now his responsible for keeping it financially healthy. One day he would take over completely, the only one in his family to do so. None of his siblings had been interested in law, so it had fallen on him. Not that his dad had expected him to do it. Yes, he had hoped, but he also wanted his children to follow their hearts.

His older brother and two older sisters had gone in completely different directions. One sister was a nurse, his brother was a plumber and the youngest of his sisters was a stay at home mum. She loved being at home with her children. So his dad had placed all his hope on Geoff joining the firm.

It was times like this he wished his mum was there to talk to, but she'd been gone for almost ten years now. She'd died of cancer and watching her fight it every step of the way right until the very end had been one of the hardest events he'd ever endured. It had almost destroyed his father, watching the woman he'd loved slowly die in front of him. He hadn't had another relationship since and at times Geoff wished he would find someone. He knew Mum wouldn't want him to be alone and had asked him to find someone after she was gone. Yet, his dad hadn't. He still loved his wife.

Hearing a sound behind him, Geoff turned from the window, seeing Clara walk into the room. Looking at the clock, he realised she'd been up there for a little over an hour.

"How is he? Did he say anything?" he asked her as she sat down.

"You know I can't divulge certain information to you?" Clara waited until Geoff reluctantly nodded. "Good. You were right about the depression and that it's not all related to his friend Adam's death. It goes further back than that. He's agreed to continue to see me and write in the journal, but it will be a slow and difficult journey for him." Leaning towards Geoff, Clara continued. "You need to appreciate that, Geoff. This is going to be hard on both of you. He will need your support and, more importantly, your understanding. He's going to behave erratically. One minute he will appear happy and the next he will lash out in anger." Clara gave him an assessing look. "Are you ready for this?"

Geoff pursed his lips, nodding. "I knew this wasn't going to be easy for him. Any advice you give me will help."

"Alright, here's a list of books that will help. They've been written by people who went through what you're about to." Clara stood as she prepared to leave. "I'm going now. I've got to take the boys to practice. Good luck and remember you are doing something worthwhile here, no matter how hard it might get. I'll be here next Monday to see Ben again. We've agreed on six o'clock. Call me anytime you need advice or even if you just want to talk."

"Okay, I'll see you then, and thanks, Clara. I really do appreciate this."

"You're welcome, Geoff. Take care."

Geoff walked Clara out and then went back into his study to stand by the window again. At last it felt like they might be getting somewhere.

※ ※ ※

Ben woke to the sounds of Geoff moving around downstairs. Pulling back the curtain, he squinted at the bright sky, realising that it was now morning. He'd fallen asleep pretty quickly after the doctor had left. He closed his eyes and covered them with his hand thinking about how he'd behaved towards Geoff. He knew the man was trying to help him and he should apologise, but he struggled to think of a way to say the words. His stomach churned when he thought about apologising and he had to take several deep breaths before it settled.

It didn't help that Geoff was so damn hot. Yeah, he'd noticed. Every time he saw him he noticed. Tall with black hair and those grey eyes that seemed to notice everything. Kind eyes, Ben had noticed.

New Beginnings

Never judgemental, but annoying as fuck. Always trying to help him. Ben groaned, rolling over and hiding his face in the pillow. He shouldn't be noticing how attractive Geoff was. The man was trying to help him and there was nothing else to it. Or maybe he was only helping him so he could fuck him. Ben groaned again. Sometimes it was like he was constantly arguing with himself. Maybe he was delusional. Ben snorted. That'd be about right, wouldn't it? He was fucking delusional.

He realised that he felt hungry for what must be the first time in days when his stomach started to rumble. Could have been the fact that eating some food yesterday had reminded his stomach what food was and now it had woken with a vengeance. He could practically hear it scream 'feed me!' He would go downstairs when Geoff left for work and then he could avoid seeing him and feeling even more guilty than he already did.

When the house had gone quiet, Ben got up and went to the bathroom to take a leak before walking downstairs and into the kitchen. He stopped at the threshold when he saw Geoff sat there, cup in hand, reading the paper.

Geoff looked up and smiled at him. "There's fresh coffee over there. Help yourself to breakfast." Geoff looked back down at the paper and started reading it again.

Ben walked in slowly, rubbing his clammy hands on his pants and grabbed a cup from the side before pouring himself some coffee. He had to hold it with both hands when he noticed how unsteady they were. Looking at the counter, he could see the breakfast cereals had been left out with a bowl and spoon next to them. He was about to leave when he heard his stomach growl. There was a slight cough behind him and he knew Geoff had heard it too.

Grabbing the bowl, he poured some cereal and added milk before sitting down opposite Geoff at the island, looking at the open doorway that led back to his room. Glancing at Geoff, Ben was once again reminded of how attractive Geoff was. How he was too good for Ben.

Swallowing, Ben realised he wasn't hungry now. He glanced back up at Geoff, noticed him smiling at him and quickly looked back at his bowl again. His face heated as he fiddled with the spoon in his hand before putting it down.

"My brother and his family are coming over for dinner tonight. Would you like to join us? My brother has two boys, so it should be fun." Ben looked up at him then quickly glanced away, avoiding eye contact. He picked up his bowl and cup before walking out of the kitchen. No, he didn't want to join him and his family. Why remind him of what he didn't have anymore? He paused at the bottom of the stairs before walking back into the kitchen. He owed him an apology and he would give him one, no matter how he felt. He stood and watched as Geoff rubbed his hands over his face.

"Sorry, about yesterday. The soup." He didn't wait to hear what Geoff had to say so Ben left the kitchen and slowly walked back up the stairs.

New Beginnings

Chapter Five

Geoff checked on Ben a couple of times throughout the day, but he was either sleeping or not talking. He'd taken lunch up for him and was glad to see that he'd tried some it. He might not have eaten it all, but it was certainly an improvement on how he'd been eating previously.

He was now in the kitchen cooking for his brother Harry, his wife Louise and their two sons, Charlie and Finley. He hadn't seen them in a few weeks with everything that had been happening and was looking forward to catching up with them.

Geoff loved his nephews, even when they were throwing tantrums. Seeing them often made him think about having children of his own. When, he didn't know. There was no one special in his life and he worked long hours.

Sighing, Geoff looked over his kitchen. He'd spent a lot of money on it because he loved to cook and tonight he was making spinach and ricotta cannelloni with garlic bread and a salad. For the kids, who were going through a fussy eating stage, just simple pasta and cheese sauce.

He put the cannelloni in the oven to cook and checked the time. He still had time for a quick shower and to change his clothes before they arrived. Running upstairs, he paused outside Ben's room before knocking and walking in. He found him in the same position he'd last seen him in. Curled up on his side facing the wall. The only difference now was that the journal was open and he could see some writing inside.

"Ben, my family will be here soon. I've done Italian. Want to come down and join us?"

Geoff waited a couple of minutes, but after getting no response, closed the door and went into his bedroom. He paused and sat on the edge of his bed looking at the wall that divided his bedroom from Ben's.

When Ben had come down to the kitchen that morning, Geoff had seen it as a positive step forward. Now, however it seemed like they had gone back to the start again. Clara had said this would happen but to witness it left a heavy feeling in Geoff's chest. Sighing, Geoff grabbed some clean clothes, leaving them on the bed, and went into his en suite. Ten minutes later he was out and getting dressed when he heard the doorbell go. Fuck, he should have known they'd be early.

Rushing downstairs, he opened the front door to be grabbed by two sets of small arms. "Uncle G! Unca G!" was shouted at him at the same time by both boys.

He laughed, reaching down and hugging both of his nephews. Charlie was the eldest at six and Finley the youngest at four.

"Sorry we're early but they didn't want to wait any longer." Louise smiled as she spoke to him. "Come on, you two. Let's get inside where it's warm."

Louise and Harry herded the children into the hallway and Geoff closed the door before following them through to the kitchen. Watching them with the children he couldn't believe how lucky his brother was. Louise was biracial and had beautiful caramel skin and dark chocolate eyes. The boys had taken her skin colouring but had their dad's grey eyes. Harry just looked like a slightly older version of him.

"Something smells good. Watcha cookin'?" Harry asked him as he attempted to get the boys' coats off of them. "Wait! Coats and shoes off before running around Uncle G's house." He shouted after them as they took off at breakneck speed laughing.

"You have moved the valuables, right?" Harry said to him as he heard the sound of more laughter echoing through the house.

"Yep, learnt that one early."

"So, whatcha cookin?"

"I would apologise for him, but you know what he's like when it comes to food," Louise commented as she managed to grab hold of Finley and get his coat off. "Shoes please, Finley."

"Aww, Mum." Finley pouted, sticking his bottom lip out and looking adorable.

"Now, Finley."

Geoff watched Finley throw himself dramatically onto the floor before trying to get his shoes off without undoing them. He managed to pull one off and somehow rolled onto his back in the process. Squatting down in front of him, and trying not to laugh, he helped him up then took his other shoe off. "There you go."

"Ta, Uncle G!" Finley shouted, jumping up and running after Charlie.

"We'll get Charlie in a minute. Where's this Ben then?"

"In his room, where he virtually lives." Geoff grabbed a couple of mugs out of the cabinet and poured them both a coffee, before passing them over. "Clara came over to see him last night and has agreed to help him. He actually came down this morning and had some breakfast, so I'm hopeful, but I know it's going to take time."

"Has there been any update about this Adam?" Harry asked him.

"None. The investigation appears to have come to a standstill. There have been no more attacks either."

"Has he talked to you at all about any of it?"

Geoff shook his head sipping from his mug, "No, and if you see him, please don't mention it. I'm not sure how he'll take it if he knew you both knew about his past."

"I wonder why he ended up on the streets," Louise mused. "I'm not sure what the boys would have to do before I did something like that. I wonder if his parents have been looking for him. They must be so worried." Louise looked at Geoff.

"I thought the same thing, Lou, but even knowing his surname, I've been unable to find out any information. The police have confirmed that he wasn't reported missing, so maybe when he left home he was old enough to do so. There's so much I don't know."

"Give it time. Charlie!" Harry suddenly shouted as he watched his son skid on his knees across the kitchen floor. "What have I told you about doing that? Coat and shoes, now."

Grumbling, Charlie took his coat and shoes off and threw them on the floor before running away again.

"Sorry, Geoff," Louise muttered as she watched the two boys chasing each other around the house, screaming and shouting as they went.

"It's nice to see them having fun. Knowing how much mess they make, I thought we'd eat in here."

"Learned from the last time, have you?" Harry smiled at him as he spoke.

"Yes. I didn't think the dining room was ever going to recover. It was like a disaster zone after they'd finished." Geoff turned to Harry, asking, "I mean, did they actually eat anything or did they just use the food to decorate the room?"

"Welcome to my life, bro," Harry muttered, slapping Geoff on the back.

Geoff snorted, opening the oven to take the cannelloni out and put the garlic bread in. He placed it on the counter along with the salad he took out of the fridge. "Who's driving?"

Harry sighed. "It's my turn tonight."

"Wine, Lou?"

"Absolutely." She answered with a wide smile.

Geoff took a bottle of white out and poured a couple of glasses for Lou and himself.

"Right, I'll start to gather the little demons for dinner. Should only take thirty minutes or so," Harry said sarcastically as he walked out of the kitchen, shouting their names.

"He loves every minute of it." Geoff smiled at Louise.

"Yes, he does."

Harry wasn't far off on the how long it would take and eventually they got the boys to sit down to eat. They'd only been sat there a few minutes when Louise spoke.

"Hi. You must be Ben. I'm Louise, Geoff's brother's wife. Are you going to join us? There's plenty of food."

Geoff turned to see Ben stood at the door, staring at his feet. He nodded before walking over and sat further down the table away from them. Harry caught his eyes and raised his eyebrows before mouthing, "We'll talk more about this later."

Yes, Geoff knew exactly what they'd be talking about. His brother might not be gay but he wasn't afraid to say when he thought a man was attractive and clearly this was what he was thinking now. Geoff nodded back at him and then turned to watch Ben.

Louise had handed him a plate with some food on it. "These two are our sons. Don't let the innocent looks fool you though. This is Charlie next to me and that's Finley sat next to his Uncle G."

Ben smiled a little when he heard 'Uncle G.'

"And I'm Harry, this idiot's brother."

"I'm the nicer one," Charlie attempted to say around a mouth full of food.

"No, you're not. I am!" Finley shouted at him.

"No, I am!"

Finley grabbed some food from his plate and threw it at Charlie.

"What are you two doing? Stop it right now!" Harry ordered them.

Of course, they listened, and Charlie threw food at Finley in retaliation.

"What did I just say?" Harry shouted as he stood up from the table.

They both ignored him and continued to grab food from their plates and throw it at each other.

"Why you little shits!" Harry told them as they ran off from the table.

Everyone could hear Charlie shouting 'little shits' as he ran around the kitchen with Harry chasing him. Louise dropped her head into her hands, sighing deeply.

"More wine, Lou?" Geoff asked.

"Sure, yeah, why not." Turning to Ben, she added, "I'd like to say that they're usually well-behaved but I'd be lying."

"You're not going to hit them, are you?" Ben asked her in a small voice.

Lou gasped. "No! Why on earth would I do that? Though the naughty step might make an appearance."

Geoff looked sharply at Ben. That one comment had told him a lot about what Ben had been through when he'd lived at home. He'd bet anyone that Ben had been hit when he was younger and it wasn't a one off. If he'd only been hit a couple of times, he wouldn't have made any comment about it.

Harry, with Lou's help, eventually got both boys sat down to finish their food, and by the end of the meal, Charlie and Finley had calmed down somewhat.

"I'm sure they're wearing more food than they've actually eaten. I think Finley's using it as hair gel," Geoff commented as he stood to start clearing the dishes away.

"Yeah, we try to recycle our food," Harry said dryly as he helped Lou try to clean the boys up. A task that wasn't made any easier by the pair of them wriggling around constantly.

Geoff was surprised when Ben came over to him with some of the plates. He wanted to know if he was right and before he could stop himself, he asked him, "Did someone hit you, Ben?"

Ben stopped what he was doing and looked at Geoff, swallowing. "What? Why d'you ask?"

Geoff shrugged. "You made a comment to Lou about the boys whether they would be hit for being naughty, so have you?"

Geoff watched as Ben's face hardened, his eyes narrowing and knew he'd made a mistake. He shouldn't have spoken.

"What the fuck has it got to do with you?"

Geoff held his hands up in front of him passively. "I don't want to cause an argument. I was just asking. I'm sorry." He spoke as calmly as possible, trying to pacify Ben.

"Well, don't fuckin' ask. It's none of your business what they did to me!" Ben dropped the plates onto the counter.

Ben seemed to realise what he'd just said and Geoff watched as he clenched his fists, jaw tensing.

"It's alright, you know. No one here is judging you for what's happened in the past," Harry told Ben.

Geoff groaned when he heard what Harry said. He knew Harry was trying to help but he could have done without him opening his fucking mouth. He rubbed his eyes, watching Ben warily, waiting for him to explode.

Ben looked at Harry, eyes bulging, mouth falling open. "You know! How the fuck do you know? Did he tell you?" Ben pointed at Geoff. "Did he tell you what I did to survive? Sucking cock and getting my arse fucked. What right did he have to tell you anything about me?" Ben screamed at Harry.

"Hey, calm down. You've got something to say, fine. But now isn't the time and you're upsetting my children," Harry told him flatly.

Both boys had started to cry when Ben had raised his voice and Lou was trying to calm them down.

"Fuck it. I'm gone."

"Ben, wait..." Geoff watched as Ben stormed out of the kitchen and a few seconds later heard the front door slam shut.

"Harry, I'm so sorry. Come on boys, it's alright now, everything's fine."

Geoff helped Lou and Harry calm the boys down. When they'd stopped crying, Harry pulled him to one side. "Go. He needs you right now."

"How can you say that after what he did?" Geoff asked, raising his eyebrows and grabbing Harry's arm.

"Because he's hurt. It looks like he was starting to trust you a little and now he probably feels you've betrayed him. He needs you, whether he knows it or not. Go, we'll lock up."

Geoff stared at Harry, seeing the sincerity. "I owe you one. I mean it, thanks."

"Go. We got this. Call me, and let me know what happens."

Geoff went over and gave Lou and the boys a hug, then quickly left. He had no idea where he would have gone, so grabbed his phone and called Seb. After quickly explaining what had happened to Seb and Tom, they both agreed to meet him near to where Tom and the others used to live.

It took him almost forty minutes to get there, and when he did, he found Seb and Tom waiting for him. He could see straight away that Tom was pissed. He held himself rigidly, hands in his pockets, glaring at Geoff as he approached them.

"Look, before you say anything, Tom, I know it's my fault. Okay? I shouldn't have asked him anything about his past, but we all seemed to be getting on alright. He'd come out of his room and was sat with my brother's family while we all ate." Geoff shook his head. "I should have known better."

"You shouldn't have said anything!" Tom virtually shouted at him, taking a hand out of his pocket to point at him.

"I know, Tom, and again, I'm sorry."

Tom continued to glare at him before he walked away. Geoff looked at Seb who was frowning at Tom's back when Tom turned and walked back towards them. "We've checked inside and new squatters live there who haven't seen him. I'll tell you where he used to go and we can split them between us."

They kept in touch but after searching for well into the night they hadn't found him and the people that Tom had spoken to hadn't seen him either. They met up where they had first started; the abandoned house. Both Seb and Tom looked exhausted with Tom also looking upset.

"I'll search again tomorrow. Someone may have seen him that wasn't out tonight." Tom offered before Geoff could say anything.

"I'm so sorry, Tom." Geoff glanced at his shoes, shaking his head. He'd been an idiot. If only he'd kept his mouth shut.

"Look, I know you're trying to help."

Seb wrapped an arm around Tom. "Come on, let's go home and try again tomorrow."

"We'll meet up in the morning. Go home and get some sleep. You both look like you need it."

After saying their goodbyes, Geoff got into his car and sat staring out the window. God, how stupid could he have been to bring up Ben's past? He smacked the steering wheel and cursed. He'd well and truly fucked up.

New Beginnings

Chapter Six

Geoff met Seb and Tom the following morning and they looked about how he felt. Both had dark circles under their eyes and they looked washed out. He'd barely slept as he thought of all the possible scenarios that could occur. Ben could be injured or attacked or doing drugs. When his alarm had finally gone off, he reckoned he'd had around two hours sleep in total.

They discussed where they were going to search and again split up the area and went their separate ways. They kept in contact continuously as the day progressed and Geoff could hear how despondent Tom was becoming every time he spoke to him.

Night was falling and Geoff was doing a final drive around the areas Tom had informed him Ben used to work. Seeing movement out of the corner of his eye, Geoff slowed the car, twisting in his car seat, looking back.

Ben. He was approaching a car that had pulled up beside him. As he leaned into the window, Geoff put his car into reverse and sped back down the street. Slamming the brakes on, he opened the car door and ran over to Ben. Ben was now walking around the front of the car.

No fucking way.

"Get in the fucking car." Geoff ordered Ben, grabbing Ben's sleeve and spinning him around to face him. Looking at the driver, he told him, "Fuck off."

He dragged Ben back to the car, who fought him every step of the way, cursing up a storm.

"Get the fuck off me," Ben screamed. "Bastard. I was working!"

Throwing him in the back, Geoff ran around to the front of the car, jumping in quickly and slamming the car locks on. Putting the car in gear, Geoff drove as quickly as he could, eager to get home.

"What the fuck are you doing? I left you! Why are you here? I had a job!" Ben grabbed the handle, trying to open the door.

"What, letting some random stranger have your arse? Some fucking job!" Geoff was furious. When he'd seen him stood there, a red veil had descended and wasn't going to lift anytime soon.

"It's my life! I'll do what the fuck I want with it!"

"I've obviously got it wrong then. I didn't realise selling your body was a good life. What do you think? Should I join you on some random corner? How much would I earn?"

"You're too fucking old."

"Really? I thought I looked good for my age." Geoff gripped the steering wheel tightly, knuckles going white.

They continued to trade barbs with each other until Geoff pulled onto the driveway outside his home. He stopped and got out, grabbing Ben before he could run off. He hauled him into the house and upstairs, shoving him into the shower. Throwing him to the floor he turned it on and blasted him with cold water.

"Fuck man, that's fucking cold." Ben shouted as he jumped at the cold temperature of the water.

"Clean yourself up. You fucking stink."

"You're just like him."

"Who?" Not getting an answer, he continued, "Come on, Ben, who am I like?" He stood there with his hands on his hips, waiting for Ben to answer his question. Geoff watched Ben look away, avoiding his eyes. "Clean up and I'll see you downstairs. Get some clean clothes on as well."

Geoff walked out of the bathroom, closing the door behind him and ran his hands through his hair as he stood in the hallway. He didn't know if he'd just made things worse or not, but he knew he couldn't let him get into that car. He was positive that would have set him further back and any progress they had made, no matter how small, would have been ruined.

He looked back at the bathroom door listening to the sounds of the shower and raised his hand as if to knock on the door. He paused when he realised what he was about to do. He dropped his hand, shook his head. Turning, Geoff walked down stairs.

※ ※ ※

Ben stood shivering under the shower, fists clenched, jaw hard, gritting his teeth. He stared holes into the tile wall thinking about what Geoff had just done to him. He was pissed off. How dare Geoff come along and drag him off like that? Who the fuck did he think he was? Bastard treating him like a little kid.

Turning the temperature on the shower up, Ben waited for the water to heat up. He struggled to get his wet clothes off, the jeans difficult to peel down his legs. They were heavy with the added weight from the water. He threw his wet clothes on the floor and smirked. Let Geoff clean that shit up.

Finding some body wash and shampoo, Ben cleaned up. He then stood under the spray, eyes closed as the water ran down his face, warming his skin. He stayed for as long as possible under the spray, hoping it would piss Geoff off. He wanted Geoff to feel like he did.

Eventually, Ben turned the shower off, opened the shower door and grabbed a towel. After quickly drying, he went to his room and put on some clean clothes. Geoff had gone shopping for him when he'd first arrived and had bought him what he had needed, which had been everything.

As he walked downstairs, heat flushed through his body and Ben ground his teeth together. His grip on the banister tightened and he looked down to see that his knuckles were turning white. How dare Geoff come after him and drag him into his car, shove him into a freezing shower and order him to clean up.

Walking into the kitchen, Ben stopped. Geoff was sat at the counter, looking defeated. He was staring into his cup with his shoulders slumped and with one hand in his hair while the other held his head up. Some of the anger Ben held disappeared as he watched Geoff. Hearing Geoff sigh, Ben walked into the kitchen, took the chair opposite Geoff, and sat.

"I was worried about you. Were you safe?" Geoff asked him, glancing up at Ben then back at his coffee.

"What? You want to know if I let anyone fuck me? Want to know how many blow jobs I gave? What I charged?"

Geoff sighed again shaking his head and took a mouthful of his coffee. "I just want to know if you were safe. I'm not the bad guy here. I want to help you, but I can't do that if you won't let me." Sighing yet again, Geoff took another mouthful of his drink. "I know you've had a hard time. I don't know the details and Tom hasn't said anything. I understand you don't want to talk about it and I'm not asking you to. I gave you the journal for that. If you want to talk to someone then talk to Clara, Dr Rimmer." Ben watched as he rubbed a hand across his jaw. "I don't know what to say or do to get through to you, so you tell me. What should I do? Do you want to go back to living on the streets? Do you want to go back to selling yourself to survive? Is that what you want?"

Ben sat, staring at Geoff, who stared back. Did he want to leave? Part of him wanted him to leave and another part wanted him to stay. Maybe he should leave, it's what he deserved. After his parents and then Adam, Ben knew he didn't deserve any happiness. Staying here, he benefited from Adam's death and he shouldn't.

Standing, he walked out of the kitchen and went into his bedroom, where he gathered his belongings, packing them in a bag. Walking back into the kitchen, he watched Geoff take in his bag and exhale slowly before standing and walking over to him.

"Okay, so this is what you want? Just know that I'm here if you change your mind. Do you need any money?"

Ben shook his head and walked out of the kitchen. As he neared the front door, he heard Geoff behind him.

"Stay safe, Ben."

Ignoring the comment, Ben opened the front door, stepped through then closed it slowly behind him. Slinging his bag over his shoulder, he started the long walk into the city.

Once he'd made it, he found the first Off License and bought a litre bottle of whisky. He hadn't told Geoff that he'd taken some money;

he'd notice it was gone soon enough. Finding an alley, he threw his bag down and sat on the ground next to it. Ben opened the bottle, taking a large mouthful, coughing as the liquid burned down his throat.

Shivering, Ben continued to drink from the bottle. The cold from the ground penetrated his clothing and Ben wrapped his coat around him tighter. Eventually, Ben forgot about the cold and the drop in temperature as night approached.

As he proceeded to get drunk, Ben thought about a conversation he'd had with Tom, where he'd told him to take a chance with Seb. To get away from this life and start over. He'd told him if he could he would. Yet, when he'd had the chance, he'd walked away.

Ben snorted. Of course, he walked away. He could hear Derek in his head, telling him how shit he was, how worthless, a waste of space. He could still feel the blows on his head and his back that would accompany the words when Derek was screaming at him. He could still hear his mum laughing as she told Derek to hit him harder and beat some sense into him and make him a man.

Taking another long swig from the bottle, Ben coughed again, his eyes watering against the sting of the alcohol hitting the back of his throat. Why couldn't he forget about his parents? Why did he let them ruin his life?

Maybe he should write some of this down. What did it matter if he did? He rummaged through his bag and pulled out the journal and stared at it. Taking another drink, he opened the journal to the first blank page and folded it back. He looked at the page. Could he do this?

※ ※ ※

New Beginnings

Almost a week had gone past and Geoff hadn't seen or heard from Ben. He understood and accepted that it had been Ben's choice to leave but wondered if he could have done or said more. It was the fact that he'd asked questions that had caused Ben to storm out of the house in the first place. Then when he'd given him the option to stay or go, he'd left anyway. Maybe Ben wanted to be on the streets. Maybe that was the life he desired? Geoff didn't know.

Speaking to Clara had eased some of the worry he felt. If this was what he had wanted to do there was very little Geoff could have done to stop it. He understood this, but it didn't mean he had to like it. He'd spoken to Seb about it as well and had asked him not to say anything to Tom. Seb hadn't liked that, they didn't keep secrets from each other, but Seb had understood the reasons why. If Tom had found out that Ben had left, seemingly for good, he'd be out looking for him and Tom was finally moving on from that part of his life.

Maybe this was what Ben needed. Maybe being back on the streets would remind him what he had given up. Geoff sighed, scrubbing his face. What the fuck did he know? He wasn't a psychologist. He was simply throwing random ideas and thoughts around.

Rubbing his face, Geoff sighed. He'd barely slept since Ben had left. Seeing his reflection in the mirror reminded him of that fact. His skin was pale and he had dark shadows under his eyes. His concentration was shot which meant Geoff struggled at work. And right now he needed to be able to focus on his current case.

"Geoff." He looked up to see Seb stood in front of his desk, having entered his office without him noticing.

"Sorry, I was miles away."

"Yeah, I knocked a couple of times and you didn't respond. Have you heard anything from Ben?"

Geoff looked out of the window. "No. I guess you can't help

someone who doesn't want it. You know that Seb."

"Yeah, I do. But my relationship with Tom is different to yours with Ben. I've known Tom for years. You two are just, or were, starting to know each other."

"I know this, Seb, course I know it," Geoff muttered in frustration, leaning on his desk.

Seb shifted, causing Geoff to look up at him, noticing the colour on Seb's cheeks. "Do you like him?"

Oh, now he knew why Seb was blushing. Did he like Ben? He certainly found him attractive; he couldn't deny that. But, he didn't know him. How did you know if you liked someone when you hadn't had the chance to get to know them?

"I'm not sure. I don't really know him. Do I find him attractive? Yes, I do." Geoff paused before asking Seb, "Do you think he's out selling himself?"

"I don't know. God, I hope not, but I don't know what else he would be doing. Given his background, it's hard to think of him not doing it. He doesn't have any money, does he? So what's left? Stealing from people." Seb glanced away, sighing. Looking back at Geoff, he added, "Let's be honest. We both know he's probably turned back to prostitution. It's what he knows."

Geoff nodded grimacing, silently agreeing with what Seb said. He leaned back in his chair, running his hands over his face. "I guess so. Like you said. It's what he knows. I've looked for him, but I don't know all the places he would go to. I'm at a loss as to what to do now. It's not like I can go to the police and report him as missing. I gave him the option and he chose to leave."

"Yeah, the police probably wouldn't be able to do anything. I've also been out looking. I've been telling Tom that I've had to work late. I don't know what more we can do on our own. I think we need to let the others know. They know the areas they worked better than we do and they know the other people out there too."

Geoff sighed. Seb was right. They needed to tell the others. "Yes, I think your right."

Seb pushed the chair back and stood up. "I'm gonna get back to it. I'll see you later, alright?"

"Yes, okay."

Geoff watched Seb leave the room and turned to stare out of the window again. Seb had looked as defeated as Geoff felt when he'd left Geoff's office and Seb was right; they needed to let the others know. They had no idea where Ben could be or where he might be working, if he had gone back to that.

Being realistic, Geoff knew Ben had returned to prostitution. Seb was right. He had no other income available, so the only thing he knew how to do was sell himself. Geoff sat back in his chair, looking up at the ceiling.

What the fuck was he going to do?

❋ ❋ ❋

On Saturday, Geoff visited his brother Harry's family. He hadn't seen them since the fallout at his house and Geoff wanted to catch up and find out how they were. He'd been worried about his nephews as they'd been upset by the shouting at his.

Geoff spent the afternoon being a climbing frame for them and generally entertaining them. He babysat for a couple of hours when Harry and Lou went out, enjoying every minute of it. His nephews were a funny, crazy pair. By the time Geoff left for home, he was tired but happy.

Harry had assured him that they hadn't been upset about what had happened. Merely concerned for Ben and had asked after him. When he'd explained what had happened, Harry had been alarmed and concerned and had offered his help to try and find him. Help that Geoff was grateful for but refused. Harry had his family to look after and Geoff saw Ben as his responsibility even though he knew he wasn't.

Driving home, Geoff thought about what he was going to do later. He'd been invited out on a date but didn't feel up to it. Not like the man wasn't attractive because he was. He simply couldn't find the energy or the desire to go.

Entering the house, Geoff walked into the kitchen to put some coffee on when he realised there was a fresh batch waiting. He stopped, listening to the sounds of the house, hearing the shower on in the bathroom above.

Fuck! Who was in his house?

Grabbing the cricket bat Geoff kept behind the front door, he slowly walked upstairs, hands sweating, heart racing, trying to make as little noise as possible. Standing outside the bathroom, he gripped the bat tightly and closed his eyes briefly, taking a deep breath in, and slowly reached to open the bathroom door when he heard the shower shut off. His hand froze in the air. Shit, how was he going to get in the room now? He stood outside, bouncing on the balls of his feet thinking about what he was going to do next when the door swung open and he stared into Ben's shocked face.

"Fuck man, you scared the shit out of me!" Ben slapped a hand on his chest, gasping.

Geoff gaped at him. "I did? Imagine how I felt when I walked into what I thought was an empty house to find the coffee made and the shower on!" He shouted at him, the adrenaline still coursing through him.

"Oh, okay. I should have thought of that. I'm sorry. Let me get some clothes on and we can talk."

It was only then that Geoff realised that Ben only had a towel wrapped around his hips. He looked at his chest and watched droplets of water run down it. Clearing his throat, he stepped back to let him past and glanced away. "I'll meet you downstairs," he murmured before quickly jogging down the stairs. As he walked back into the kitchen, he let out a breath of air he hadn't realised he had been holding. Oh yeah, he was attracted, which just complicated things.

Why had Ben returned? Geoff poured two coffees and waited for Ben to appear. He'd hoped but had never expected to see Ben again. After the way he'd left, he'd assumed that was it. Even when he had been out looking for him, part of him had thought that he wouldn't see him again. So, why was he here now?

Grabbing his phone, he sent a message to Seb to let him know Ben was back. Seb's reply came quickly. He'd just finished telling Tom what had happened and Tom was furious with him for not telling him sooner.

Geoff swore and called Seb and he answered on the second ring. "It's okay now. I've told Tom that he's back." Geoff could hear raised voices in the background and was ashamed of himself for causing it.

"Look, apologise for me. Tell him it was all my idea," Geoff told Seb.

"Pfft, already done that. Don't worry, he'll get to you soon enough."

Geoff turned when he heard Ben enter the room. "Got to go. Speak to you tomorrow." Hanging up, he walked over, picked up the coffees and nodded towards the living room. He walked away, knowing Ben would follow. Sitting down on the sofa, he watched Ben hesitate at the doorway before pulling himself together and walking in. Geoff sat silently waiting for Ben to speak.

Taking in Ben's appearance, Geoff frowned. He hadn't noticed in the bathroom but now it held his attention. Ben's face had bruises on the jaw and cheek. Dropping his gaze, Geoff looked at Ben's hands seeing the cuts and swollen knuckles. How many fights had Ben been in? Were there other bruises that Geoff couldn't see?

Glancing back up to Ben's face, Geoff noticed the hollowness of his cheeks, the sunken eyes and dark circles underneath. What had Ben endured?

The silence stretched between them and Geoff could feel the tension build in the room. He was about to speak when Ben faced him.

"I'm sorry. I just want to say that before I say anything else," Ben muttered.

"Were you alright? And how did you get in?"

"Spare key. Was I safe? That's what you want to know, isn't it?" Ben glanced down at the cup in his hands. "I can't blame you asking about that. I've been living here for weeks with you trying to take care of me and me throwing it back in your face. I want to tell you everything, I do, but it's hard, so just give me a minute, okay? There's a lot to tell."

Geoff nodded and sipped his coffee as he waited.

And waited.

Ben cleared his throat then nodded. "Alright. When I was five, my dad left home. My Nan moved in to help as Mum seemed lost. I guess, looking back now, she was devastated that he'd left. Mum remarried soon after and Nan moved out. She didn't like him. I couldn't understand why because he was always nice to me, but after he'd moved in, things changed. I was six the first time he beat me."

"What?"

Chapter Seven

Ben fidgeted on the sofa, struggling to get comfortable. His stomach churned and he bit his lip, a light film of sweat breaking out over his skin. His eyes darted around the living room but not at Geoff. He was nervous about talking, about bringing up his past and dusting it off for Geoff to hear.

Having spent a week or so back on the streets, Ben had learned one thing: he didn't want to be back there. He'd hated it. The cold, the damp, the smells. The hardness of the ground against his body. Having to curl up as tightly as possible to make himself look smaller and less of a target. Listening to other people doing drugs or throwing up or screaming and shouting. Sleeping with one eye open all the time, trying to stop people from stealing his belongings.

The fights. He'd had a lot of fights. He'd been unable to control his anger and had lashed out at anyone who had tried to touch him or take his belongings. His anger. It had burned inside of him, like a volcano ready to erupt at the slightest provocation. That first night he'd been so drunk he hadn't cared what had happened to him, but when he'd sobered up, he'd started to realise what a huge mistake he'd made.

The time at Geoff's house had made him realise that he probably wouldn't survive living on the streets. It wasn't that he'd lost his street smarts; he'd just lost his will to continue doing things that way. He knew he had issues with his past. The constant arguments in his head, the constant mood swings. Fighting anyone who tried to help.

Ben looked at Geoff's shocked face, taking in Geoff's wide eyes and parted lips. "Six. Derek, my step-dad, hated me. I didn't know it at the time. I would cry asking what I'd done wrong, begging him not to hurt me and asking my mum for help."

"What did she do?"

"Nothing. It got to the point that she would be urging him on." He paused gathering his thoughts. "The beatings weren't too bad. It was the things they said to me or when they would lock me in the cupboard." He paused. "I'm still afraid of the dark," he whispered.

He stopped again, taking a deep breath. Talking about this was far harder than he had anticipated.

"I lost count of the number of times I was at the hospital with various injuries. They always had a reason why I had them and social workers didn't seem too interested. I had clean clothes, didn't look neglected. One time they beat me so bad, I wanted to die. I still have the scars on my back." Ben broke off, swallowing. His throat burned and his eyes itched. Blinking rapidly to clear them, Ben continued, "They wouldn't go to the hospital because the injuries looked exactly what they were. He'd taken his belt and had used the buckle end to hit me with it. My head and back. I remember crawling under my bed, crying as I tried to get away, but my mum pulled me out so he could continue. I don't remember what made them stop, but they didn't hit me for a long time after that."

He stopped talking, again overwhelmed by the emotions remembering his past brought up. Coughing to clear the lump in his throat, Ben tried to compose himself. He needed to get through this. He'd tried not to think about this, about his past, but he'd found himself lost, more so since Adam's death. When he went back on the streets, he only thought about his past. It was like he had opened the door to those memories, and he was unable to shut it again. Like a dam that was breaking. He jumped when he felt Geoff's hand on his leg.

"That's enough for now. We can talk some more later or whenever you're ready. There's no rush. It's been a difficult week for you. Eat something then go to bed. You look shattered."

Ben looked up at Geoff and tried to show him how determined he was to finish what he had started. He hardened his jaw, shaking his head.

"I didn't do anything. I want you to know that. I thought about it, I even got into some man's car. It was when I heard him rip open the condom wrapper that it finally sunk in what I was gonna do. I pushed him away and got out of the car and ran as fast as I could. I realised that once I started, I wouldn't stop because it's so easy to fall back into doing something you're used to. It's not so easy to walk away and try something new, even if you know it's better for you. For so long I thought I was worthless, a waste of space, but you showed me something different. You made me feel like I mattered. So let me finish this bit, okay?"

Geoff moved over and sat down next to him. "Alright. I'm here."

Ben smiled at him before continuing. "As I said, they didn't beat me for a while. Then one night he came into my room and tried touching me. He had his hand over my mouth so I couldn't make any sound. I fought him as hard as I could and luckily kneed him in the balls." Ben stopped, rubbing his face. "He never tried touching me again, but the beatings started again and became worse, if that was possible. They would starve me, never enough for it to become obvious, and the things they would say to me. I was blamed for everything going wrong in that house, for my dad leaving, for Derek never working, there never being enough money. You name it, it was my fault. Derek liked to have me stand naked while he put his fags out on me."

"Jesus," Geoff whispered. "How did you get away?"

"Once I did my exams, I waited for them to get drunk one night, and I packed my bags, grabbed the money I'd managed to save and left. I grabbed some things I could sell, pawning them for the extra money. I stayed with my Nan. I never told her what had happened, but I knew she wouldn't say anything to them. She wasn't talking to them anyway, hadn't for years. I had to change jobs as they started turning up, causing trouble.

"A few months before my seventeenth birthday, Nan died. She hadn't been well for a while, so I knew at some point I might have to leave, but I'd hoped she would have been around for longer than she was. I'd missed her growing up. Her hugs." He smiled slightly to himself thinking about her. About her warmth and love. "Anyway, she didn't own the house she was living in, so I couldn't stay there and I ended up on the streets. I preferred that to going back to them. I had some money, but not enough and I ended up selling myself. Then I met Adam, and not long after, Tom."

Ben finished his coffee and sighed. It was a start, a good start to exorcising his demons.

"When did you last have something to eat?" Ben looked at Geoff, surprised at how close he was. He'd forgotten that they were sat next to each other.

"Er ..." He couldn't remember the last time he had eaten. Was it two or three days ago?

"If you can't remember that, it was too long ago. Come on, I'll heat up some soup for you."

Ben stood following Geoff as he walked into the kitchen and watched as he heated some soup up in the microwave. When it was finished, he placed the bowl in front of him along with some thick bread and a fresh mug of coffee.

"Thanks, Geoff."

"I think that's the first time you've used my name."

Ben looked up at him, the spoon paused midway to his mouth, seeing the smile on Geoff's face. "Huh? Really?"

"Yeah." Geoff smiled at him. "It's nice to hear." Ben watched Geoff suddenly look away, running a hand through his hair. Clearing his throat, he continued speaking. "I'm going to call Seb, let him know everything's alright."

Ben nodded and continued to eat. He hadn't eaten anything halfway decent in days and was now ravenous. His clothes felt looser due to weight loss, and he couldn't afford to lose any more. He didn't have a lot of weight on him after living on the streets.

He could hear Geoff talking in the other room and tried to ignore it but could hear his name being mentioned. He was disgusted with himself for the fact that he'd put so many people through a shit week while he'd run away from, well, himself. He had also run from the people who were trying to help him. That reminded him of Geoff's family.

When Geoff walked back into the room, Ben asked him about his nephews. He'd made them cry the first time they had ever met him.

"They're fine. I was around there today, so my back can testify to how well they are." Geoff grimaced.

"Used you as a climbing frame." Ben smiled.

"Oh yeah. I'm going to feel it tomorrow, that's for sure. Have you finished?" Geoff asked him as he stretched.

"Yeah, thanks." The last word came out garbled as he suddenly yawned.

Geoff chuckled. "Go to bed. Get a good night's sleep and I'll see you in the morning. A word of warning though."

"Er, what?" Ben asked him, stomach twisting.

"Tom's angry with you, so expect a visit from him at some point tomorrow. I've been warned he'll probably shout at you. He's apparently been doing a lot of that since Seb told him you'd left."

Ben looked down at the counter shifting on the stool as his face flooded with heat. He bit his lips as his chest tightened and he swallowed. If Tom was coming over here and shouting at him made him feel better, then Ben would take it. Ben nodded to Geoff. "I understand."

"Go to bed. You look dead on your feet and don't worry about it. Once you've spoken to Tom, everything will alright."

Standing, Ben said goodnight and walked up to his room. The bed smelled freshly made as if Geoff had been expecting him to come back and had been keeping it ready for him. Stripping, he got in and curled onto his side. For the first time in days, Ben felt safe and within minutes was asleep.

※ ※ ※

Geoff was in the kitchen making breakfast when he heard

movement upstairs. A couple of minutes later, Ben walked in, yawning and rubbing his eyes. His dark hair was stuck up in every direction possible, and he had creases on one side of his face, courtesy of his pillow.

"Morning. Sleep well?" Geoff asked, smiling at the state Ben was in.

"Like the dead."

"I'm making pancakes for breakfast. Want some?"

"God, yeah. I love pancakes." Ben smiled at him, dimples showing.

Geoff laughed, telling him, "My nephews love them too. Whenever they stay over, it's the first thing they ask for. I've got some fruit in the fridge. Can you get it for me? Oh, there's some syrup in the cupboard too."

"Oh wow. You sure know how to feed a guy."

Geoff stacked some pancakes on a plate and placed them on the counter next to the bowl of fruit Ben had put there. "Tuck in."

Geoff paused, watching Ben load his plate up with pancakes, then pour copious amounts of syrup over the top before placing fruit on the pile as well. He raised an eyebrow when he caught Ben looking at him.

Ben flushed and shrugged. "I really like pancakes."

Geoff pursed his lips. "It sure does look that way. Don't worry, I'm making more."

He thought he heard a garbled 'good' before he turned back to the cooker and poured more mix into the pan. It was good to see Ben eating and being more open with him. He needed to smile more because when he did, it lit up his whole face and Geoff could admit he was a sucker for those dimples.

Before Ben had left, he'd been moody, withdrawn and noncommunicative and now, he seemed more at ease, more open. Maybe his experience back on the streets had opened his eyes, and he'd realised that he had the chance to escape from it.

Geoff wasn't stupid to think that the worse was over. If there was anything he'd learned from Seb about his relationship with Tom was that there were good days and bad. Though Tom did appear to be doing better now. Geoff could understand a little about the reasons why Ben had behaved the way he had. It couldn't have been easy growing up the way he had. More like pure hell. Never knowing if you were going to be beaten or starved or locked in a dark room. The emotional abuse can be just as bad if not worse than the physical abuse. No wonder Ben had such low self-esteem and felt worthless.

Putting the pancakes on another plate, Geoff switched the cooker off and sat down to eat when he realised that Ben had virtually finished the first pile of pancakes. He looked from the plate to Ben and back again. Ben just shrugged, smiled sheepishly, and then carried on eating.

"I've got a lot of catching up to do," Ben mumbled between mouthfuls of food.

"No, no, it's fine," Geoff muttered more to himself. There'd easily been enough on the plate for both of them, and he'd made more because he'd seen how many Ben had piled on his plate. At the rate Ben was eating, Geoff would have to make more.

Geoff kept furtively glancing at Ben as he ate. He really was very attractive. He was underweight, there was no denying that, but Geoff could see how good looking Ben was. And those dimples?

But, why had Ben come back? What had he experienced when he'd been out there? What had he seen or done?

"I can see you, you know. What's up?" Ben asked, glancing up at Geoff.

"I'm glad you're back, but..."

"You want to know why I came back?"

"Yeah." Geoff nodded. "Why the sudden change of heart? When you stormed out of here, I thought for sure that was it. I was never going to see you again. You barely acknowledged me when you were here and, as I said, I'm glad you're here now, but what made you come back?"

"I had a lot of stuff to work out, a lot of things going on in my head. I was arguing with myself. Always second guessing myself. No, don't call for the padded wagon yet." Ben smiled slightly. "But part of me wanted to come back, and yet a part of me felt like I didn't deserve it." Ben shrugged. "I guess that's something from my past, you know, how they treated me. I've always felt useless like I couldn't do anything right. I suppose if you hear it said often enough you start to believe it and I certainly did." Ben looked Geoff in the eye. "I didn't feel like I belonged here. I'd thought about killing myself, but that didn't work out so well, and that seemed to fuel this feeling of how shit I was. I guess though, deep down I wanted to live, and it was only when I was back on the streets that I realised it. I couldn't go back to how things were. Sleeping rough and letting strangers fuck me for a few quid."

Ben paused, as if he was trying to find the right words. "I remember speaking to Tom about it. When Seb wanted him to move in, and Tom had said he couldn't do it, that he didn't feel like he could leave us and that he didn't deserve it. I told him that he had a chance for a new beginning, and he should take it. Yet, I couldn't do the same thing."

"I wrote in the journal you gave me. I felt stupid when I started, but once I did, I couldn't stop. It all just kinda poured out of me. You know what I mean?" Geoff nodded before Ben continued. "I was sat in this alley and there was a kid, younger than me, shooting up. I knew then that I had to leave. Adam was dead, and that could easily have been me. Nothing I do will change the fact that Adam isn't coming back, and I don't want to end up like him. I want a life, a chance to be someone. That's not selfish, is it?" Ben asked Geoff, staring at him.

Geoff paused for a moment before he spoke. He hadn't expected Ben to say so much, especially after everything he'd told him the night before, so he chose his words carefully. "It's not selfish. You've been through enough for someone your age."

"And you have no problems with me coming back here? It's alright, isn't it? If not, I can leave, I'll understand. I wasn't exactly nice to you, was I?" Ben asked, biting his lip.

This was not the conversation Geoff was expecting to have this morning. He didn't want Ben to leave. If anything, he wanted to get to know him more. What Geoff saw now was someone he could like, maybe even something more? But, he had to go slowly and carefully. As he'd told Ben, he'd been through enough.

"I want you to stay. I kept the bed made in the hope I'd find you and convince you to come back."

"You looked for me?" Ben asked with wide eyes.

"Both Seb and I. We didn't tell Tom at first—that's why he's so angry now. Seb wanted to tell him, but I convinced him not to. I owe them both an apology."

Ben messed with the cutlery, biting his bottom lip again. "I'll apologise to them. I caused this mess so it should be me." Ben took a deep breath in. "There is something I want to do."

"What?"

"I'd like to get tested. I know the others have and even though I was always safe, I'd like to make sure. Could you help me arrange it?" Ben looked flushed when he finished speaking and wouldn't look

Geoff in the eye.

Geoff smiled. It was good to see that Ben was concerned about his health. Different to his behaviour before. "Yes, of course I'll help. Do you want to see Clara again?"

Ben nodded. "Yeah. Even though I only spoke to her once, I think I need it. She was nice to me."

"I can arrange that for you as well. Anyway, have you had enough to eat?"

"Yeah, I'm stuffed now." Ben leaned back, patting his stomach.

"Go, get changed and we can do something today if you want."

Ben smiled. "I'd like that."

"Think about what you want to do and we can go out."

"Hey, can we meet Tom and Seb? I'd like to apologise to them."

"Sure, I'll call Seb now and see what we can arrange."

Geoff watched Ben leave the kitchen and smiled. Ben's behaviour had done a complete turnaround, and he appeared more settled. The atmosphere in the house felt lighter and there was less tension in the air.

He phoned Seb, and they arranged to meet for lunch in the city. Once the call was finished, Geoff went upstairs to get ready and plan their day.

Chapter Eight

They spent a couple of hours walking around Manchester City Centre, getting to know one another before meeting Seb and Tom for lunch. As they walked up to the restaurant, Geoff saw them standing outside waiting. He felt Ben tense up beside him, slowing slightly when he caught sight of them, and Geoff turned to look at him.

"Hey, don't worry. Tom was concerned for you too," Geoff reminded him.

"I know, but I feel like I let him down. I told him to go to Seb when he had the chance, yet I couldn't do the same thing when I had the chance." Ben bit his lip, glancing at Tom and Seb.

Geoff grabbed his arm and stopped him, turning him to face him. "It will be fine. Sure, he's angry, but he'll get over it. Go up to him and apologise and everything will work out."

"Hope you're right," he heard Ben mutter before he continued walking towards them.

Seb turned and waved to them as they got closer, and Geoff saw him lean over to Tom and say something to him. Tom frowned and then shrugged before pulling Seb in for a kiss, smiling at him.

"Before you say anything, I want to apologise for the way I've acted." Ben avoided their eyes, looking anywhere but at Tom and Seb. Ben shoved his hands in his pockets, shoulders slumped.

Tom stepped forward, pulling Ben in for a hug, whispering something to him that Geoff couldn't hear. He saw Ben nod his head a couple of times before stepping back and smiling at Seb. "Hi."

Seb smiled. "Should we go in? It's not too warm today."

Geoff held the door open and they all walked inside. They only had to wait a minute before being led to a table by the window. Geoff sat next to Ben and put his hand on Ben's leg when it bounced up and down. Ben murmured 'sorry' to him and stopped moving his leg.

"So how are things going, Tom?" Geoff asked him.

"I've decided to go to college, finish my education. I might do A-levels after that. Matt and Luke have already chosen the courses they want to take, and I thought I should finish mine too. You need a good education nowadays, and I don't want to sponge off --"

"It's not sponging!" Seb interrupted him.

"It is to me. Anyway, I'm looking for a job, but with no education, it's been difficult." Tom shrugged.

The waiter came over at that point and they ordered their drinks. Geoff had a job in mind for Tom but wasn't sure if he'd be receptive or not. He didn't want Tom to believe he was only offering him the job because of his relationship with Seb, but he knew being employed would improve Tom's self-esteem and he needed to feel better about himself.

"I have an offer for you, Tom. I've had to let an employee go, they weren't working out, so I need someone I can trust to fill in for me. It's minimum wage, but the real downside is--" he paused for effect-- "you'd see Seb several times a day."

Tom looked at him sceptically as he cocked his head. "What is it?"

"Filing."

"Filing?" Tom repeated, frowning.

"You can do it until you go to college, plus it'll look good on your CV."

"Why would you offer me this job?" Tom asked warily, pushing back from the table and crossing his arms over his chest.

Seb dropped his head in his hands before looking at him. "Maybe he just wants to offer you a job."

"Look, I can't help being the way I am. I'm still not used to people helping for no other reason than because they want to."

"So, you'll take it then?" Geoff asked. "You can start Monday and work the same hours as Seb, that way you don't have to pay for transport."

Tom frowned at him. "Hang on, I haven't agreed to it yet."

"But you will. You know me, Tom. Take the offer."

Tom leaned back in his chair, searching Geoff's face. Geoff had grown accustomed to people staring at him, so this didn't concern him. He could see Seb looking more and more horrified the longer the staring contest continued. Eventually, Tom nodded.

"Okay. I'll be there tomorrow."

"Glad we got that sorted. Shall we order? I'm starving, and I know Ben can eat!"

Ben snorted out a laugh. "It was a few pancakes!"

"A few? That pile was for both of us, but I saw how many you piled on your plate so I made more."

"Really? That small pile was for both of us?"

"What's this?" Seb asked them, looking between the two of them.

"When Ben decided to get up, he spotted the pancakes and had the majority of them. Not that I minded, I was glad to see him eating, but he can certainly put food away."

Ben blushed, muttering, "Shut up."

Geoff laughed, shaking his head as he looked over at him. Ben looked back at him and also smiled, making his dimples pop out. Geoff paused, staring at him. Damn, Ben was gorgeous.

They were interrupted by the arrival of the waiter with their drinks and, after quickly looking at the menu, they ordered food.

Lunch went well, and Geoff was able to observe the changes in Tom. He'd come a long way from that boy he'd first met and that had only been a couple of months ago. Obviously Seb was good for him. And as for Seb, he was the happiest Geoff had ever seen him.

Once they finished, they left the restaurant and said their goodbyes and Geoff and Ben walked slowly back to where he'd parked his car.

"That went well," Geoff commented to Ben.

"Yeah, it did. I thought for sure Tom was gonna go off on one, but he seemed a lot calmer. Not that he was a hothead anyway, but it's nice to see him looking happier. I know he came to see me, and I pretty much ignored him."

"He knew you had things to work out."

"He was always trying to look out for us and keep up safe. He would pass on any news he'd heard, you know if we shouldn't go to a certain area for a while or avoid one altogether. He's not much older than me, but he cared about us."

"I forget you're only eighteen."

"Almost nineteen." Ben shrugged as he flushed.

"When?"

"Fifteenth of March."

"That's only a couple of weeks away."

"Yeah."

A party would be nice for Ben. "We could have the four of them over for a meal if you want."

"You would do that for me?" Ben asked, eyes wide.

"Sure. Wow, to be nineteen again." Geoff chuckled to himself.

"You're not that much older than me."

"Sixteen years older, Ben."

"Too young for you, then." Ben seemed horrified when he realised what he'd said, his hand covering his mouth. "Oh fuck, forget I said that. Please."

Geoff stopped walking and looked at Ben. He'd thought this attraction was one-sided, but it would appear that wasn't the case.

"Too old for you?" Geoff said as he watched Ben's flush deepen and stare at his feet. "Come on, let's go home."

Ben began walking but avoided making eye contact with him. Geoff sighed as they reached the car. Leaning over the roof, he waited for Ben to look up at him. When he did, he smiled. "It's okay. I know I'm old and wrinkly. Not hip enough." Putting his hand on his chest, Geoff sighed dramatically. "Be still, my poor heart."

"Shut up. Man, you're embarrassing," Ben murmured, rolling his eyes.

Geoff laughed as he unlocked the car and they got in.

※ ※ ※

Monday he was back at work updating some of the cases he was handling when he heard a knock on his door. When he looked up, he saw Tom there, hesitating in the doorway glancing around Geoff's office.

"Come in, Tom. Don't stand on ceremony. Take a seat." Geoff smiled at him pointing to the chair opposite.

Tom came in and sat in front of him, messing with the cuffs on his shirt, then the collar. It was when Tom was pulling at his pants that Geoff spoke.

"You don't have to be nervous, you know. Relax. Today I'm going to show you the file room that needs a lot of work, and I mean a *lot* of work. You can then get to know the place and meet the people who work here."

"Yeah. Look, I don't want to mess things up, and I don't want this to affect Seb's job here."

"Whatever happens with you and Fosters will have no impact on Seb's job here. Don't worry about that. If it doesn't work out, at least we tried, right? You also need to sign some forms, you know DPA, data protection act, et cetera, and your contract."

Tom sighed, nodding before a wry grin crossed his face. "Nerves." He shrugged.

"Let's go down to where you'll be working and I'll show you around."

Geoff stood and, with Tom following, walked him towards the file room. He paused before opening the door then waved Tom in ahead of him. He almost walked into Tom, he'd stopped so abruptly in front of him. He watched Tom look at the room slowly before he turned to face him.

"This is...fuck...sorry. I don't know what to say. I hate to ask, but what system was being used?"

Geoff looked around the room and winced. With everything that had been going on with Ben, he hadn't been aware of the fuck up that was occurring. He'd employed someone to ensure that the room was kept tidy and organised, as at any time a file may be needed, and he'd done nothing of the sort. There were files stacked together, drawers hanging open with files spilling out. Some files had had their paperwork scattered across the floor and he groaned when he realised just how large the task would be to get the room back in full working order.

"Yes, the man I had employed just shoved them in, or not, as it would appear. Of course, I would have found out sooner, but I've been distracted with the situation with Ben and I didn't pay attention. Staff tried to mention there was a problem, but it stupidly slipped my mind. It was only last week that I finally did something about it when I came in here and found him smoking a joint."

Tom chuckled, shaking his head. "Okay. What system did you have in place then?"

"What do you know?"

Tom looked at him incredulously. "You're just asking me this *now?*"

Geoff rubbed the back of his neck with his hand. Tom shook his head walking further into the room, stepping over spilled paperwork or bending to look at some files.

"Lucky for you I do have some experience. My parents had their own business. Corner shop. I did stock taking, inventory and spreadsheets. When I was older, I took on a Saturday job because it actually paid and I wanted money."

"Good. Come over here and I'll explain how it should be set up."

Twenty minutes later and Geoff had shown Tom everything he needed to know to get the room organised. Tom had asked sensible questions that had surprised him. He had a lot of knowledge, and he found himself wondering why his parents would kick him out for being gay. He was clearly intelligent, probably smarter than he realised. As he was getting ready to leave, he heard Tom speak.

"Sorry. What was that?"

"You and Ben. Do you like him?"

"Sure, he's a nice young man." Geoff frowned facing Tom.

"'Nice young man.' Okay. Do you like him? As in like him. You know, fancy him, find him attractive."

"What?"

"I'm not blind. I saw the way you were both looking at each other yesterday. I think it's cool. He deserves someone nice like you."

"Hang on, back up. Looking at each other? How were we looking at each other?" Geoff asked, shaking his head. How had he been looking at Ben? And, he hadn't noticed Ben looking at him either.

"Like you wanted to eat each other." Tom grinned widely when he told him.

"No, you're wrong and Ben's been through enough as it is. He doesn't need any more complications right now."

"Do you like him? Yes or no?"

"Tom. You are an employee--"

Tom waved a hand at him. "Blah, blah, whatever. Ben is my friend. We've been through a lot of shit together. I'm looking out for him. You can understand that, can't you?"

"Yes, I understand what you're trying to say."

"So..."

What was the harm in admitting it? He wasn't going to pursue a relationship with Ben. "Yes, I do find him attractive."

"It's the dimples, isn't it? Damn, I wish I had dimples." Tom shook his head, sighing dramatically then smiling at Geoff.

"I think Seb loves you just the way you are, but the dimples are nice." Geoff paused before adding, "I'm not going to pursue anything with Ben. He needs time to adjust and get used to his life as it is right now. He might want to go to college and meet new people, make new friends. I'm over ten years older than him."

"So? What if it's you he wants?"

"How would I know that he really wanted me or if this was a form of gratitude for helping him?"

"Fuck, Ben doesn't roll like that. He's always been aware of who he is. He might not have thought very highly of himself, but he isn't stupid either. We met a lot of people doing what we did. You'd be surprised at who would pay for a quick fuck. We met men from all walks of life. None of them cared about us. They didn't offer us a way out. Once they were finished, they were gone." Tom stared intently at Geoff. "You've been there for him no matter what shit he threw your way, and you haven't asked for anything in return."

Geoff nodded. "Let's see."

Tom continued to stare at Geoff until he too finally nodded. "Okay. I'll get started then."

"I'll send Seb down when it's time for lunch," Geoff told him, walking towards the door.

"Yeah, alright, and Geoff?"

"Yes?" Geoff asked, twisting to face Tom.

"Thanks."

Geoff smiled. "You're welcome, Tom."

Geoff stood and watched Tom work, rummaging through paperwork and files, muttering to himself. After a few minutes, it became apparent that Tom had forgotten that he was there. Leaving him, he walked back to his office and found Seb waiting for him.

"Well?" Seb asked him as he entered his office.

"He knows what he's doing. I left him muttering about the place looking like a disaster zone and how he was obviously needed." Geoff smiled. "How was he last night?"

"Nervous but excited. When we got back yesterday, he was telling Matt and Luke about the job."

"I told him you'd get him for lunch, but I think he was already distracted at that point."

Seb laughed a little then sobered. "He's smarter than he thinks. He just needs to gain a little confidence in himself."

"Well, hopefully this will help him."

"Thanks for this. I appreciate what you're doing."

Geoff waved him off. "I needed someone, so he's helping me. Now go. I've got a lot of work to catch up on."

When lunchtime came, Geoff called home to see how Ben was doing before calling the detective in charge of Adam's murder to see if there were any updates. He wanted to find closure for Ben as he was aware of how guilty he felt over it. The detective didn't give him much information, but it was clear that they had nothing concrete to go on. It looked like they would need to have another attack before they could continue with the investigation, which was frustrating. Other people would have to suffer before they were likely to catch whoever was committing the crimes.

Clara was happy to hear from him and willing to see Ben again. She agreed to start the sessions at Geoff's house and, when Ben was ready, move them to her clinic.

Geoff checked on Tom a couple of times throughout the day, but Tom hadn't noticed as he was too engrossed in his work. There had been files all around him, and he had been sat on the floor in the middle of it all with a pen and paper taking notes.

It was six when he heard the knock on his door and saw Tom and Seb stood there. Leaning back in his chair, he smiled at them before asking Tom, "How did you find your first day?"

"Fuck, it's a mess down there, and it's gonna take me a while to sort everythin' out, but it was good. I have to ask though, how did he get away with it for so long? What was he doing?"

Geoff knew he was responsible for the state things had gotten in, but he had been preoccupied with Ben. He also knew that wasn't a good enough reason because, at the end of the day, he was the one in charge.

"Nothing, by the state of things."

"We're going home now, but I wanted to remind you of the time as I know how you are when you get lost in one of these cases," Seb told him.

"Yeah, thanks. I had lost track of the time. Go. I'll see you both tomorrow."

A few minutes later, he closed down the programme he'd been

working in and switched off the computer. Grabbing his belongings, he walked out of the office, saying goodbye to some of the staff still working. It wasn't uncommon for staff to work late into the night, especially if new information came to light in a case or if they had deadlines to meet.

It took almost an hour to get home, and when he finally walked in, the first thing he noticed was the delicious aroma. Walking into the kitchen, he found Ben stood in front of the cooker, stirring something in a large pan.

"Wow, that smells wonderful. I didn't know you could cook."

Ben shrugged as he continued to stir. "I had no choice growing up, but I'm kinda glad for it now. I had a look at some of your recipe books and chose an Italian dish. There's wine in the fridge along with a salad."

"Let me get a shower and change then I'll be down to help."

Ten minutes later, he was back in the kitchen, asking what he could do.

"It's only pasta, but the sauce is homemade."

"I appreciate this. It's nice to come home to a cooked meal, but I don't expect you to do this."

Ben shrugged. "I know, but it makes me feel useful, and that's a feeling I haven't had in a long time."

Geoff nodded, then spotted Ben's journal on the counter. "Have you been writing?"

Ben looked over to the journal, colour flooding his cheeks before nodding. "Yeah. Can't seem to stop now I've started."

Geoff saw the faint blush on Ben's cheeks and decided not to ask any more questions, but he was glad that he was writing about his experiences. From what Ben had told him, it sounded like he hadn't had a great childhood.

"It's ready now. Can you pass over the plates please?"

Geoff passed the plates to Ben and then went to the fridge to get the salad and wine. He put them on the counter then grabbed a couple of wine glasses and cutlery. Sitting down, he started to eat and then moaned as the sauce hit his taste buds. Damn, Ben could cook!

Ben chuckled. "That good?"

"It's fantastic, Ben. You can always taste the difference between a jar and something that's been homemade." Geoff ate some more before speaking again. "Tom started today."

"How was he?"

"Well, he was nervous at first, but once he started, he was in a world of his own. I went to see him a couple of times, but he didn't even notice me." Geoff laughed, remembering the look on Tom's face as he was working. "He was pulling files out and muttering to himself scratching his head."

Ben nodded as he continued to eat. Geoff watched him for a couple of minutes before he too continued eating. After finishing, Geoff stood and started putting the dirty dishes in the dishwasher.

"I can do that."

Geoff looked up from where he was knelt in front of the dishwasher and shook his head. "No. You cooked, so I'll clear the table. Go and sit down while I do this."

He watched Ben hover over him before he eventually walked away. Geoff smiled, watching Ben go. It was nice to finally see some of the real Ben coming out. There would be setbacks. Hell, he'd seen it with Seb and Tom, and there was no denying the fact that they clearly loved each other.

He walked towards the living room and leaned against the door frame, watching Ben stare out of the window. "Want to watch some TV?" he asked him as he pushed away from the door frame.

Ben jumped before he looked over at him and gave him a shy smile. "No, thanks. I'm gonna go to bed actually."

"Night then, Ben."

Ben stood and walked past him, looking at his feet. "Night, Geoff."

"Hey, is everything alright?"

"Yeah. It was nice." Ben shrugged. "See you in the morning."

Geoff watched Ben walk out of the living room before he sat down. Yeah, it had been nice, and now that it appeared Ben was going to be staying, they would hopefully have more evenings like this. Geoff hadn't been this relaxed in a long time. The one problem Geoff faced was his growing attraction to Ben. Something he would have to fight if he was going to be of any help to him.

Chapter Nine

Over the next few weeks, Ben made sure to have something ready for Geoff when he returned home from work. It felt good to be useful and to be doing something that helped him. He kept the house clean, did the washing and the food shopping with some money Geoff had left. Even though Geoff had told him not to cook every night and that wasn't why he was there, he enjoyed it. For so long he had lived hand to mouth and sometimes that had been food that had been thrown out and wasn't fit to be eaten. You did what you had to, to survive. So, cooking with fresh food? Not a problem as far as Ben was concerned.

What Ben did find hard was his attraction to Geoff. The man just seemed to appear more gorgeous with every passing day. He would find himself staring at Geoff when they ate together in the evening. It was becoming embarrassing. He was positive Geoff had noticed it as well. It was inconceivable that he could have missed it with the number of times he'd looked up to find him staring at him. Ben groaned whenever he thought about it and the fact that Geoff always had a little smile on his face afterwards.

Shaking his head, he started preparing the food for dinner that night. He had decided on cooking a chicken Pad Thai that he'd seen in one of Geoff's books. He'd never had Thai before and was looking forward to trying it. He'd bought the ingredients and had read through the recipe. He planned to start cooking it when Geoff came home.

That was another thing. He was thinking of Geoff's house as his home, yet it was only a few weeks ago that it had felt like a prison. Being on the streets for that week had opened his eyes in ways no amount of talking had done. Seeing what he had escaped made him realise that he would be a fool to go back to that way of life. That was when he'd started writing in the journal. Seeing what people did to survive. Before, he'd become accustomed to it, but seeing it fresh again made him realise that he didn't want that, he didn't want to have to fight daily to live.

He had issues, fuck knows he had them, and maybe talking to Clara, Dr Rimmer, would help some. He'd seen her that day and had agreed to continue seeing her and write in his journal. He hadn't realised how much he had blocked out, locked away somewhere in his head.

The years of emotional, mental and physical abuse by his mother and Derek. Then his time on the streets. It was true that you could switch off when working and ignore what was being done to your body or the things you had to do to someone else. His body had simply become a means of survival. He couldn't even say how many men he'd sucked off or had let fuck him. They all seemed to blur into one.

Thinking back to Clara and their session, he'd struggled to answer some of the questions she had asked. The ones where he had to look deep inside himself and reveal emotions regarding things from his past that he had hidden away. He lost count of the number of times his chest had constricted or his throat had burned and his eyes had itched.

New Beginnings

Shaking his head slowly, Ben thought about Geoff again. Yeah, he thought about being with him, but really, what chance did he have? He was used goods. The best he could do was be a good friend to Geoff until he could get himself set up. A job first, well, once Ben found out what his exams results had been, then a new place to stay.

Hearing the front door open, Ben walked into the kitchen to start cooking. Geoff walked in, carrying a box and a bag, and smiled at him.

"Hey, how's your day been?" Geoff patted him on the back as he spoke.

Ben sighed. What he wouldn't give to have Geoff come in and hold him or kiss him, but he knew better. Enjoy what he had. "Fine. I've been thinking about my exam results. I never got them, you know."

"Have you decided to go to college?"

Ben shrugged. He hadn't thought past getting a job. "I was thinking about a job."

Geoff frowned at him. "Don't you want to go to college?"

"I haven't thought about it. I just thought about a job and then maybe I could get my own place. I must be cramping your style, right? You can't bring people over and let's not forget how I was when your family came. So, yeah, a job." Ben started throwing the ingredients in the wok and checked the noodles he'd already placed on the hot water.

"You don't have to leave. This can be your place too."

"What about when you want to bring a woman over?" Surely, Geoff wanted to date someone?

Geoff snorted, and Ben looked up at him. He watched as he smiled at him. "I'm gay, so no on the women."

"Oh, I...I just assumed..." Ben stuttered, mouth falling open. Geoff didn't appear gay, but he should know better than anyone that looks could be deceptive.

"Yeah, you did. I'm not in the closet, so to speak, I just don't advertise it. I don't feel like I should have to. My sexuality is my business and nobody else's."

"Your family is alright with it?"

"Yeah, why wouldn't they be? Not all families are like Tom's. My family wasn't even bothered when I told them. My dad was like 'surrogates.'" Geoff chuckled.

"I never said anything to my family." What he wouldn't give to have had a supportive family like Geoff.

"Well, I can understand why." Geoff gave Ben a faint smile. "Anyway, what are we eating?"

"Chicken Pad Thai."

"Sounds nice. Any wine in the fridge?" Geoff asked, walking over to the fridge.

"Yeah." Ben waited a few seconds before adding, "Clara came."

Geoff looked at him from where he stood by the fridge. "Did it go okay?"

"Yeah. I'm gonna see her again next week here and then maybe go to her clinic." Ben shrugged as he told Geoff. Clara had said baby steps when it came to talking about everything that had happened to him. He'd only given Geoff a brief glimpse of what he'd been through, so he knew reliving everything with Clara would be a long and difficult journey.

He put the noodles into the wok and mixed everything together. It smelled great, and Ben hoped it tasted just as good. He grabbed a couple of plates and served the food then placed them on the counter as Geoff poured the wine.

He sat and watched as Geoff started eating, and then nodded his head. "This is great!" he mumbled around a mouthful of food. Ben started eating, watching Geoff. The way his black hair fell over his forehead and how he would glance up at him and Ben would see his grey eyes, smiling at him. Fuck, he had it so bad. He rolled his eyes at his own behaviour.

Once they finished, Geoff went over to where he'd stored the box and bag and gave them to Ben.

"What's this?" Ben asked him, tilting his head as he looked at the items.

"Happy birthday."

Ben stared at him, his mouth falling open. Geoff had remembered his birthday? He blinked rapidly when he felt his eyes itch. He wasn't going to cry.

Geoff smiled widely, showing perfect teeth. "Open them, Ben."

Ben looked in the bag and found a black cashmere jumper. He lifted the jumper up and smoothed his hands over the material. It was soft to the touch.

"Now the box."

Ben reached over to the box and lifted the lid and laughed. There, in the box, was a Buzz Lightyear birthday cake. Ben shook his head, staring at the cake.

"Want some?" Geoff asked.

Ben lifted his head, smiling widely at Geoff. "Yes, please."

They ate the cake and then cleaned the kitchen. Geoff opened another bottle of wine, and they sat in the living room, relaxing. Ben usually had one glass of wine but decided to have another one when Geoff offered. It was his birthday after all. Geoff raised an eyebrow at him, but said nothing as he refilled Ben's glass.

They sat and watched a film while Ben began to feel tipsy. Relaxed, warm and giggly. As the end credits came on screen, he found himself leaning against Geoff on the sofa.

Sitting up, Ben bit his lip then leaned over Geoff. It felt right to kiss him. He gently pressed his lips to Geoff's, closing his eyes when they touched. Geoff gasped pulling back, looking at Ben with his eyebrows raised.

Something in his expression must have given Ben away as Geoff reached over and cupped his face between his hands and pulled him in for another kiss. Their lips gently touched again and again. Ben moaned when Geoff's tongue licked across his bottom lip. He opened his mouth and tentatively touched his tongue to Geoff's. It had been such a long time since he'd kissed someone.

Their tongues slid into each other's mouths then entwined as they tasted one another. Ben moaned deeply, sliding his tongue into Geoff's mouth, trying to touch every part of it. When Geoff sucked on his tongue, Ben moaned loudly. It felt so good. The taste of Geoff was overwhelming.

He felt himself being lowered onto the sofa, Geoff moving on top of him. He jumped slightly as the cold leather touched his bare skin, gripping Geoff's biceps tightly. Ben moaned again when Geoff kissed and bit his neck before licking back up to his jaw. He kissed Ben on the lips again and moved away.

Ben opened his eyes looking at Geoff, who was smiling down at him. He didn't know why he'd stopped. He frowned up as he asked him, "Why did you stop?"

"You've had a drink and I want you to be sober next time this happens, because Ben? This--" Geoff pointed between the two of them-- "This is going to happen again."

Ben was pulled up from the sofa and stood next to Geoff. He

wobbled before he was able to stand up properly. Maybe Geoff was right. Now, he was stood up he felt light-headed and the room was spinning.

Geoff palmed his face as he leaned down and kissed him again. "I'll see you in the morning."

Ben watched Geoff walk out of the room and slowly sat back down on the sofa. He groaned dropping his head in his hands. He'd been so stupid. What was he thinking kissing Geoff? And what had Geoff meant? This would happen again? Did that mean he wanted to be with Ben? He knew what he'd done, how he'd survived and yet he still wanted him. Could Ben believe him? He started chewing on his thumbnail thinking about what would happen now. Something he wouldn't know about until the morning. And Ben wasn't sure if he wanted the morning to come.

※ ※ ※

Ben woke the next morning to sunlight streaming in through the curtains. It pierced his eyes, and he screwed them tightly shut, grimacing at the stab of pain and pulling the bed covers up over his head, his stomach protesting. That second glass of wine had not agreed with him!

He rolled onto his side hearing a knock on the door. The door opened, and he poked his head out to find Geoff stood there wearing a pair of jeans and nothing else. His dick started to stir in his boxers as he looked at Geoff's chest. That surprised Ben. He couldn't remember the last time he'd had an erection.

Man, Geoff was built. No eight pack, but a nice six pack. Ben's heart started to race in his chest and he blushed, pulling the covers up so that only his eyes and head stuck out. He was on the thin side and had started to put some weight on now he was eating regularly, but still...

"Breakfast's downstairs when you're ready."

Ben groaned, pulling the covers back over his head as he heard Geoff laugh. He heard a clunking sound and looked up to see a cup by his bed.

"Tea. Thought you might need it."

Ben groaned again, then pulled himself up into a sitting position on the bed and squeezed his eyes shut, waiting as his stomach protested. Once it had settled, he reached for the tea and closed his eyes as he sipped it and couldn't contain the moan when it hit his tongue. It was the best cup of tea he'd ever tasted!

"Five minutes and I'll be plating up. A proper English breakfast. Just what you need if you've had a couple too many the night before."

"Okay. I'll be there in a minute. Thanks for the brew." Ben smiled at him, taking another drink.

"Anytime."

Ben heard the door close and glanced over to it, leaning back against the headboard. What had he been thinking when he'd kissed Geoff? Yeah, Geoff had kissed him back, and he'd said they'd talk about it when he was sober, which was now, but what did that mean? Had he heard him right when he said that something would happen between them? And more importantly. Was Ben ready? He chewed his bottom lip, looking at the cup in his hands. He took a deep breath then released it slowly. If he was going to get any answers for his questions, he needed to get up.

He grabbed some pants and a shirt and, after a quick visit to the bathroom, found Geoff in the kitchen. There was a plate of food sat waiting for him. "Thanks."

Geoff nodded towards the plate and Ben started to eat. He'd felt a bit queasy before he'd started to eat, but that soon eased. Tucking in, he wasn't aware Geoff was talking to him until he practically shouted, "Ben!"

He looked up quickly, "Huh! Sorry. What were you saying?"

"Last night..."

"Sorry about that, it was the drink," Ben interrupted him glancing away. He really didn't want to look at Geoff.

"Oh, so you didn't mean to kiss me then?" Geoff frowned at him as he asked the question.

"No."

"That's a shame."

"What? Why?" Ben asked as he looked back up at him.

"I find you attractive, Ben, from the moment I first saw you lying in that hospital bed. There was something about you, but I didn't offer you a place to stay in the hopes that I could get laid. So, I hope that pass last night wasn't you trying to thank me for letting you stay."

"No! No, it wasn't." Ben shook his head.

"So, it was just the drink talking." Geoff stared intently at him. "No attraction at all."

Ben felt his face heat and looked down at his plate, playing with his cutlery. Should he tell him? Geoff had said he found him attractive, but what if it was some trick? He didn't want to get hurt. But Geoff seemed different.

Ben gulped before shakily saying, "I like you."

"I hoped you did. What do you want to do about it?"

"You're asking me?" Ben squeaked at him.

Silence filled the room. Eventually, Geoff spoke. "Let me tell you what I like? I thought about this last night and decided to be honest with you and let you decide. I'm dominant in bed. I like submission, total submission." Geoff leaned back on his chair. "You need to think about that."

Ben gaped at him. Dominant, like hitting people. What the fuck? "You like to hit people?" The last thing he wanted was someone to hit him.

"There are many aspects to BDSM. It's not all about pain, Ben. Yes, some people do enjoy that aspect, but others don't. I have been to clubs, and I'm currently a member of one, but I haven't been recently." Geoff took a drink of his coffee. "Some scenes I watch and others I don't. I like to be in control, maybe a little light spanking, but not serious pain. For me, both people involved have to enjoy it, and hitting someone and causing serious pain for that person to get off isn't something I enjoy. Plus, there's always safe words."

"Safe words?" Ben frowned again. He had no idea about BDSM other than people hitting other people.

"Yes. A word that a submissive can say if they want things to slow down or stop. The submissive is always in control. When they use their safe word, everything stops."

"So, no torture then?"

"No. As I said, the submissive is in total control, strange as that may sound to you."

"What do you like?" Ben asked him.

"Are you sure you want me to answer that question? You need to think about what I've said. I can show you a couple of websites that will educate you on what is involved. There are extremes, but I don't like that." Geoff paused, staring intently at Ben. "Would you like to have a look?"

"Would you always want to do that?"

"You mean would I like vanilla sex, as well?" Ben frowned--vanilla? He nodded. "Yes, but I like the other too."

"Oh."

"Oh." Geoff smiled at him. "Think about what I've said and we can talk later. If you decide that's not your thing I'm alright with that as well. I want to have a relationship with you, Ben. I can wait until you're ready. The last thing I want is for you to rush into something that you're not ready for."

Ben watched Geoff clean up and thought about what he'd said. Geoff wanted a relationship with him, but it wouldn't just be ordinary sex. Could he do that after everything he'd been through, and if he couldn't, would Geoff willingly give up that part of himself to be with him?

"I'm going into the city today. Want to come with me?" Geoff asked after he had finished cleaning the kitchen.

"Sure, okay. I'll just have a shower then I'll be ready. Twenty minutes?"

"Yeah, go. I'll see you down here."

Ben stood in the shower thinking over what Geoff had told him. He wasn't sure if it was something he would be able to do. He wanted Geoff, but BDSM? He needed to seriously think about it before starting any form of relationship with Geoff.

Ben was back down in fifteen and within a few minutes they were driving into the city in Geoff's car. Ben liked the car. It wasn't what he expected Geoff to own. A people carrier. He told Geoff as much.

Geoff chuckled. "I always wanted a sports car, but when my first nephew arrived, I realised that wasn't going to happen. I love having them over and trying to fit everything and the children into a small car just wouldn't work. So, I bought this instead."

"You have them often?"

"Yeah, I like to give Harry and Lou a break. My sister has two children also, but she moved down south when her husband was promoted, so I don't see them as often. As for Charlie and Finley, they can be a handful, but I love them." Geoff smiled.

"Have you ever wanted children of you own one day?" Ben asked him.

"Yes. I might be gay, but I do want a family of my own."

"I never thought about it. It wasn't something I ever thought I would have a chance at. I didn't expect to live for much longer, on the streets. It's not somewhere you expect to live for a long time." Ben felt Geoff squeeze his leg as he spoke.

"I guess not."

They sat in silence as Geoff drove into the city and found somewhere to park. Once he'd paid, they walked towards the centre. Ben looked at him as they walked. "What're you getting today?"

"What? Oh, it's Harry and Lou's wedding anniversary soon, so I'm looking for a gift for them."

"Have you anything in mind?"

"Nope. Nothing at all." Geoff laughed.

"How long have they been married for?"

"Er, not sure. Maybe ten years. They met at Uni and married not long after they both finished."

"So, what is ten years in married years? I mean what do you buy for ten years?"

"Don't know. Here, let me look on my phone."

After a minute or so looking, Geoff snorted before saying, "Tin."

"Tin?" Ben asked. Really? For ten years of marriage, it was tin?

"Yes. If you have been married ten years it's supposed to be tin according to this."

"Oh well. Tin of baked beans and you're sorted then." Ben smiled.

"Oh yes, I can see how happy they'll be with that!"

"I thought it was a great idea."

"Alright. I'll leave it to you to explain to Lou then." Geoff smiled at Ben.

Him tell Lou? "No thanks."

Geoff raised an eyebrow. "Wise decision. Let's go and see what we can find."

They spent a couple of hours battling the Saturday shopping crowds before they finally called it quits and left. Geoff settled on a silver picture frame and had booked them a romantic getaway to Paris for the two of them. Ben thought the holiday was a fantastic present. A weekend away, just the two of them with no children? It sounded like bliss.

When they arrived home, Geoff made lunch and then went to finish some work in his study, so Ben took Geoff's laptop and decided to look at the websites Geoff had told him about. Oh. My. God. The things that were on there! St. Andrews cross! Cock and ball torture! Whips, canes, tawses, floggers. Docking, sounding. People actually wore collars and some had leads attached and there were swings. Real fucking swings! No. Definitely not. Ben shook his head, clicking the different pictures, bringing more images to the screen.

Some of the stuff on the website didn't seem too bad. The Shibari looked interesting. The different ways someone could be tied up. Yeah, he did get a twitch when he thought about that. Maybe there were elements he would be willing to try if they went slow.

Pushing the laptop away, Ben sat back. He really did have a lot to think about.

New Beginnings

Chapter Ten

After a couple of hours, Geoff went into the kitchen and began preparing dinner. They'd had a large breakfast and lunch so he was going to make something light. He stood looking at the contents of the fridge when he heard Ben come up behind him.

"Fancy a takeaway?" he asked Ben as he continued to stare at the fridge. Nothing was leaping out at him even though it was full.

Ben shrugged. "Sure. I was just coming in to have a look."

Geoff closed the door scratching his head. "Can't decide what to cook, so thought we could have takeout. What do you fancy?"

Ben glanced at the floor then up at Geoff, smiling. "Pizza and garlic bread."

Geoff leaned against the fridge door. "Pizza, huh?"

"I love pizza." Ben smiled, flashing his dimples.

Geoff nodded. "Alright. What do you want on it?"

"Meat feast," Ben answered immediately.

Geoff grinned at Ben. "I love meat feast too. Garlic bread or cheesy garlic bread?"

"Cheesy of course. Can't have pizza without cheesy garlic bread."

"Right. I'll order while you get us a couple of beers out."

Geoff placed the order and walked into the living room. "Fancy a movie? Action, horror or romance?"

"No choice. Horror wins all the time."

"Okay, old or new?"

"Let me have a look."

Geoff made way for Ben to see the films he had. He picked out a couple and handed them to Geoff. *The Ring* and *Paranormal Activity*.

"Okay. I didn't think you would go for these two. I thought you would want more gore."

"Nah. I like the scare factor, you know. That moment when you jump out of your skin with fright. I'm not so much into the blood and guts. Seems too many films have that in now for no other reason than they can."

"I'll put *The Ring* on first then, if that's alright with you."

They'd been watching it for a few minutes when the doorbell went. Geoff got up and a few minutes later came in with some boxes. Placing them on the table, he opened them up.

"Come on, dive in."

They ate the food while watching the movie. At one point, Geoff got up and took the boxes out before he returned with another couple of beers. By the time they started the second movie, Geoff was nice and relaxed. He looked over to where Ben sat on the chair.

Patting the sofa next to him, Geoff said, "You don't have to sit over there. Come sit next to me on the sofa."

He watched Ben start to peel the label of his bottle avoiding eye contact before he finally got up and sat next to him, giving him a shy smile as he did. It puzzled Geoff that someone with as much sexual experience as Ben would be so shy around him. Maybe he was shy in general, and he'd put it aside when he'd been on the streets working. Or maybe he wasn't sure how to act now they had admitted their mutual attraction and Geoff had told him about BDSM.

Geoff pulled him closer to him and put his arm around his shoulder. He felt Ben tense up for a few seconds before he relaxed against him, leaning his head on Geoff's shoulder. They continued to watch the film, and when it ended, Ben jumped up.

"I think I'll go to bed now."

Geoff frowned at him from where he was sat on the sofa before he put his bottle down and stood up. He watched Ben bounce from foot to foot, then reached out to hold Ben's shoulders. Ben looked up at him as Geoff slid his hands up Ben's shoulders and neck and eventually cupped his face.

Leaning forward, Geoff slid his lips across Ben's. Ben gasped at the contact, and Geoff slipped his tongue into Ben's mouth, moaning from Ben's taste. He could taste the beer and Ben. Ben's tongue touched his tentatively before Ben moaned and wrapped his arms around Geoff, holding him in a tight embrace.

Geoff stepped back to the sofa and sat down, pulling Ben down to straddle his lap, not once breaking their kiss. He pushed his hands into Ben's hair and wrapped it around his fingers while their tongues entwined. God, he loved the sounds Ben was making. His moans and little gasps had Geoff's dick hard.

Biting Ben's full bottom lip, Geoff licked the sting away, smiling at Ben's gasp. Kissing along Ben's jaw, his stubble scraping against his lips, Geoff moved down his neck before he reached Ben's collar bone. Stopping, he sucked on the skin, feeling Ben's body jerk above him. Geoff pulled back, staring at the mark he'd made, and suddenly felt possessive of Ben. He liked the fact the mark was there for everyone to see.

Looking up into Ben's face, Geoff smirked at the expression on his face. Ben's eyes were hooded, cheeks flushed and his lips were swollen and wet. He looked gorgeous when aroused. Geoff wanted nothing more than to hold him down and fuck him. He watched Ben open his eyes, and he could see the lust evident in the blown pupils.

Ben leaned down and kissed him again, licking his lips before pushing his tongue inside. Geoff sucked on his tongue, feeling Ben's body jerk. When Ben started to rub up against him, Geoff thrust up to meet him, grinding their hard cocks together.

Ben was moaning constantly, and Geoff thought he was going to explode from those sounds alone. Ben was panting, his body moving and rubbing harder and quicker against Geoff's. Geoff reached down between him and started to rub Ben's cock through his jeans, feeling it twitch beneath his fingers.

Ben suddenly gasped and threw his head back crying out, his body jerking and shuddering, his hands gripping Geoff's shoulders. Geoff grinned, knowing he'd gotten Ben off. He liked being the one to bring Ben pleasure.

Ben's head dropped forward, resting on Geoff's shoulder, and Geoff pulled him close, listening as Ben panted. After a minute, Ben's breathing became steady and Geoff rubbed his cheek against Ben's hair.

After a couple of minutes, Geoff gently pulled Ben away and

smiled at him. "You alright?" he asked when Ben wouldn't look up and meet his gaze.

Ben nodded but still wouldn't look at him. He put his fingers under Ben's chin and pushed his head up so he could look him in the eyes. Ben's eyelids looked heavy, his lips swollen, skin flushed, but he also appeared embarrassed, his eyes glancing away.

Geoff didn't want Ben to be embarrassed about what they'd shared. "That was hot."

Ben blinked looking at him, wide-eyed. "Really?"

"Oh yeah. Can't wait to watch you again."

Ben flushed even more as he looked away.

Geoff reached up and cupped Ben's face, moving it so he was facing him. "Hey, don't be embarrassed. You look amazing when you come and to know I did it? Wow."

Ben frowned, moving slightly.

"Getting a bit itchy?" Geoff smiled at him.

Ben blushed. "Yeah, I am."

"Want to go to bed?"

Ben's eyes went comically wide. "You want me to go bed with you?"

Geoff laughed outright at that. "I'll do whatever you want me to do. We go at your pace."

Ben chewed his bottom lip looking down at his hands in his lap. "Er, I don't think I'm ready for that just yet. Do you mind?"

"No. Do what feels right for you. Go and have a shower and I'll see you in the morning."

Geoff helped Ben to stand before cupping his face and slowly kissing him again. When he pulled away, Ben had a dazed look on his face. Geoff watched Ben walk out of the room before sitting back down on the sofa and running his hands through his hair. He wanted nothing more than to carry Ben to his bed, strip him down and fuck him until morning. He looked down at his erection. "Just you and me tonight," he muttered.

※ ※ ※

Next morning, Geoff woke up with a hard on he could hammer nails in with. He'd dreamt about fucking Ben all night. He groaned putting his arm over his eyes. God, he hoped Ben wanted to give a relationship a try. If last night was anything to go by, then Ben did.

Geoff listened to Ben moving around and looked at the time. It was past eleven. He groaned again before he pulled back the covers and walked into the en-suite. After a quick shower, and orgasm, he dressed and went downstairs. He found Ben in the kitchen cooking sausages.

"God, that smells good."

Ben smiled at him. "Yeah. When I lived with my Nan, we always had sausage sandwiches on Sunday. Any plans for the day?"

"I have some work to finish up, and then I thought we could go out."

"Trafford Centre."

Geoff looked at Ben blankly. "You want to go to the Trafford Centre on a Sunday. Do you know how busy it'll be?" Seriously? The Trafford Centre on a Sunday?

Ben nodded. "Yep. I've never really had the chance to go before. I was always on the outside looking in. I mean, what was the point? I

New Beginnings

couldn't afford anything, and the way I dressed? Well, I would probably have had security following me around." Ben shrugged as he started to butter the bread.

"I never really thought about that in regards to you." Now he was thinking about it, and how it would have affected Ben. He realised there must have been so many things Ben had missed.

"You helped Matt and Luke out, didn't you?" Ben asked, interrupting his thoughts.

"I knew you all needed clothes, but I never thought about the why in depth."

"You never had the need to." Ben shrugged. "It was just that way for us. Whatever money we made we tried to keep for as long as possible. None of us liked what we were doing."

"I've been meaning to ask you. How did you avoid drugs?"

"I hadn't been on the streets long when I ran into Adam, and he was pretty clued up, or so I thought. I didn't know he was secretly taking. Then we met Tom and, for someone as young as us, he had his head on straight and he helped me to avoid things like that. Plus, you could see what it did to people who were taking drugs. The number of overdoses I saw..." Ben shook his head staring out of the window. "It was a way to escape. Who knows, maybe someday down the line that would have been me? You can't live that type of life for a long time. I know you see older people on the streets, but if you look closely, you can tell they have some form of habit. Most people end up developing one."

"When I've talked to Seb about this, he always expresses his amazement at how Tom avoided falling into those pitfalls. He always tells me how strong Tom is mentally."

Ben placed a plate full of sausage sandwiches in front of Geoff and a cup of coffee. "Thanks."

"You're welcome. I don't know where I would've been if it weren't for Adam and Tom."

Silence descended as they ate their food and when they had finished, Geoff cleared the kitchen. He then went to his study to finish some work before getting ready to go out. He found Ben in the living room watching TV.

"Anything interesting?"

Ben chuckled. "Nah. I forgot how bad Sunday TV is."

"Yeah, it is. Are you ready to go?" He wasn't looking forward to this at all.

Ben stood up and stretched, his shirt riding up to reveal his abs. Geoff watched and felt his dick start to get hard. Not the right time! Not when he was about to endure the torture that was Sunday shopping at The Trafford Centre. Still, a kiss would be nice.

As Ben went to walk past him, Geoff reached out and grabbed his arm, pulling Ben towards him. Ben looked up at him with his lips parted, and Geoff took advantage. He bent over and kissed him, slipping his tongue into Ben's open mouth. He felt Ben's tongue stroke along his own and moaned as Ben's taste flooded his mouth. God, he loved kissing Ben already.

When Ben's arms reached around his neck, Geoff pulled him closer, resting his hands on Ben's hips. He slowly moved his hips against Ben's, feeling Ben's erection against his own. He moved his hands up Ben's body until he was holding Ben's face. He slowly pulled back and looked at Ben. His eyes were closed, and he was panting slightly.

"Still want to go out?"

Ben's eyes opened and he narrowed them. "Are you trying to distract me?"

Geoff took a step back and placed a hand on his chest with a mock gasp. "Who? Me?"

Ben placed his hands on his hips and looked directly at him. "Yes. You. We are still going."

Geoff sighed dramatically. "If we must."

"My God. You'd think I was taking you to your execution."

"I might prefer it," Geoff mumbled to himself as he went to get his coat.

"Sorry? What was that?"

"Er, nothing?"

"Hmmm. Come on. We can have something to eat there, and I can tell you what I've been thinking of doing."

Geoff grabbed his keys and wallet and walked out to the car, pressing the fob to open it. He locked up behind him as Ben got into the car. It took them almost thirty minutes to get there and when they did it took another five minutes to find a parking space.

"Are you sure about this? We can still leave," Geoff asked Ben hopefully as he turned off the engine.

"We're here now. Come on, it won't be too bad."

"You say that now."

They got out, locked up and walked into the Trafford Centre. Almost immediately, the noise hit them. There were children laughing, screaming and crying, people talking, the music from the system overhead. People were walking in any direction and bumping into other people and not seeming to care.

Geoff watched Ben stare in awe at what he would describe as an organised chaos before he turned to him and smiled. "I'm so looking forward to this."

Geoff stared at Ben, groaning. "You're looking forward to this?" he asked as he manoeuvred himself around a group of teenagers who seemed to have set up residence in the middle of the mall.

"Yeah. I never got to do any of this."

Geoff looked at Ben. "Didn't your mum or Derek take you?"

"Why would they do that? They didn't give a shit about me."

Well, that decided it, didn't it? "Let's go then." Goof took Ben's arm and started walking towards the nearest shop.

"Can I go to all the shops?"

"Seriously?"

Ben nodded.

"You want to go into Ann Summers?"

"They sell toys, don't they?" Ben asked as he looked away, five different shades of red.

Geoff leaned down and whispered in his ear, "You want toys, do you?"

Ben shrugged, still not looking at Geoff. "I might. I don't know yet."

Grabbing his hand, Geoff forced his way through the bustling crowd. Ben pretty much went into every single shop there. It didn't matter if he was interested in what they had to sell or not. Seriously, prams? But Geoff didn't say anything. It was clear Ben was enjoying himself as he dragged Geoff around.

He had to admit, some of the toys he saw were great. They didn't have them when he was growing up, and he was tempted to buy some under the guise they were for his nephews. They eventually took a break for something to eat in the food hall, which took almost thirty minutes of queuing, and then they started again. When they came to

Ann Summers, Ben blushed and shook his head before walking on, pulling Geoff behind him.

By the time they left it was almost four and Ben was laden down with bags. Geoff had bought clothes for Ben along with other items he may need. Ben had tried to refuse but Geoff had told him to just accept it for now. He needed the things and Geoff had liked buying them for him.

When they arrived home, Ben went straight to the kitchen and started pulling ingredients out from the fridge. "Omelette sound okay?"

"Yeah. We had a large lunch. Want me to do anything?"

"Could you make a salad?"

They worked together in the kitchen and made idle conversation as they ate. Geoff cleared up and then followed Ben into the living room. The temperature was starting to drop outside, so he decided to make a fire. Once it was going, he sat next to Ben on the sofa, pulling him close.

"Did you enjoy today?" Geoff asked him.

Ben looked up at him smiling, dimples showing. "Yeah, but I wouldn't do it all the time. I feel sorry for parents trying to control their kids when out in a place like that."

"That's why I try not to go at the weekends. It always packed."

Ben suddenly yawned. "Think I'll head on up to bed. All I've done is walk around some shops, but I'm tired. I'll see you in the morning."

Geoff stood up when Ben did and pulled him in for a kiss. He gently rubbed his lips across Ben's before releasing him.

"Night, Ben."

"Night, Geoff, and thanks for today. I appreciate it."

"You're welcome."

Chapter Eleven

The next couple of weeks followed the same pattern; Ben would cook dinner for them both and keep the house clean. It gave him the opportunity to write in his journal and keep his appointments with Dr Rimmer.

Ben hadn't wanted to see anyone at first, had fought against it, but now that he was going, he had to admit that the sessions were helping. The things that had happened when he was younger, things he had shut away, were now coming out into the open, and even though they were painful, he was glad to feel finally free of them. So many incidents from his past, the beatings, being locked in the cupboard naked, the forced starvation, were all coming out.

He'd met with Tom for lunch a few times and had talked a lot about Adam. He was sure that the conversations helped both of them. It certainly helped him. The feelings of guilt he'd had over Adam's murder were slowly disappearing.

Tom had been right, well, they all had. It wasn't his fault that Adam had run off that night. They had all tried to reach out to Adam, but he hadn't wanted any help. Maybe he had become too reckless, and it had ultimately ended with him losing his life. Or it could have been the fact that he'd been on drugs. From what Ben understood, Adam hadn't been taking them for long. How the professionals knew that, Ben didn't know. Maybe toxicology reports. But Adam being on drugs had led to him taking chances he wouldn't have normally taken.

Talking to Geoff about what he thought he should do with his life, and after meeting with Tom, Matt and Luke, he had decided to go to college. Geoff was looking into him finding out what his exam results had been, and then he would decide what he wanted to study. Things he hadn't even dreamed of doing were now within his reach, and Ben wanted to make sure he made the right choices.

The situation between him and Geoff was going well too. Slow, but good. Ben wanted to take things further, but Geoff didn't seem to want to rush. He'd looked at some more websites and wanted to know more, but whenever he brought the subject up with Geoff, he would smile and say they would talk about it later.

Ben wasn't sure how much more he could take. He wanted to do things with Geoff. More than the kissing they had shared. He hadn't even come with him since that time in Geoff's living room, and he was becoming frustrated. Having an orgasm by himself wasn't cutting it anymore. He'd even talked to Tom about it when they had met up for lunch, and Tom had reassured him that Geoff was thinking of him.

They had gone to Geoff's brother Harry's home a couple of times, and they had welcomed him in with open arms. Lou was wonderful with the boys, and the boys had made him laugh so hard that his stomach ached with the trouble they caused. It was nice being included in a loving family. Something he had never experienced when living at home.

New Beginnings

So he was now sat in the kitchen deciding on how to convince Geoff to move things forward. Maybe he should tie himself up on Geoff's bed, naked. He chuckled to himself, thinking about the look Geoff would have on his face if he walked into that.

The other option was one he'd been toying with for a few days now, but wasn't sure if he had the courage to go through with it.

Submission.

The thought of kneeling naked, waiting for Geoff both excited and scared him. Part of him liked the idea of handing control over to someone else. He'd had to be in control of everything for so long that he wanted to hand it over to someone else and let go.

Ben looked at the clock, and realising how late it was getting, quickly made a vegetable chilli, and then went upstairs to shower. He dried himself and looked in the mirror. He'd put on some weight and now looked far healthier than when he had first arrived. His ribs didn't stick out as much now and his face looked fuller. His blue/green eyes had a sparkle to them now and he'd lost the pale, washed out look.

Taking a deep breath, he walked downstairs and checked the food, then knelt on the floor. God, he hoped Geoff came home soon because the floor was cold and was going to hurt his knees.

When he heard the key in the door, he suddenly tensed, muscles going rigid, his stomach turning, wondering if he'd made the right decision, but before he could get up and get dressed, Geoff walked in. He listened as he walked through the house and entered the kitchen. With his head down, the only thing he could see was Geoff's shoes.

Ben watched the shoes move away, and he listened to Geoff put his briefcase down and what sounded like his jacket coming off. The shoes appeared in front of him again, and he was tempted to sneak a peek up at Geoff to see what expression he had on his face.

"Stand."

This was it. Ben took a deep breath in and stood, keeping his eyes on the floor, like he'd read. He felt Geoff's fingers under his chin and slowly his head was raised up. When he was looking at Geoff, he saw him smile.

"Good boy."

Ben shivered when he heard those words. Good boy. It did something to him, something he couldn't quite explain. Warm. Tingly. Hard.

"Go upstairs and put some clothes on, then we'll talk about what I expect from you."

Something of the disappointment that Ben felt must have shown on his face because Geoff pulled him in and kissed him hard, before pushing him away.

"Dressed. Now," Geoff told him in a low authoritative tone, his stare intense.

Ben swallowed, nodded and quickly went upstairs to dress before racing back down. What had he done wrong? Ben was aware he didn't know everything to this lifestyle, but he didn't think he'd messed up.

When he walked into the kitchen, Geoff was serving the food and pointed to the stool. Ben sat and waited for Geoff to join him. When he also sat, Ben rushed through what he wanted to say.

"I'm sorry. What did I do wrong?" he asked, pushing his food around his bowl.

"Nothing, but I think I need to explain to you what I want from our relationship. I like to dominate, but only in the bedroom. I like total control in that aspect of my relationships. I don't expect to have control anywhere else."

"Oh. So I shouldn't have been kneeling? Oh God, I'm so sorry..." Ben dropped his head into his hands and groaned, his face flooding with heat. Ben's stomach tensed and he squeezed his eyes shut. *Please let Geoff be gone when I open them.*

"Stop," Geoff told him, pulling Ben's hands away. "You couldn't have known, but it does tell me that you might want to move forward with this. I wanted you to be sure. I don't want you to think that I expect sex because you're living here. I don't want you thinking that because of your past I'm expecting you to perform." Geoff paused, staring intently at Ben. "Are you sure you want to do this?" he asked.

Ben swallowed, looking away. The way Geoff was staring at him like he was his sole focus was a little daunting. To know that this man would have control over a certain aspect of his life? Scary, but also exhilarating, freeing. Being able to relinquish control to someone else eased a part in him he hadn't realised had been too tightly wound.

Looking back at Geoff, Ben nodded. "Yeah. I've thought a lot about this. Yes, I'm scared, but I know that I want to try this, with you."

Geoff watched him for another minute before nodding and continuing to eat. "Eat your food, Ben."

Ben suddenly didn't feel hungry, but ate some anyway. When he'd had enough, he pushed his bowl away and started to clear up.

"We need to talk about Adam's funeral."

Ben stood up from where he had been putting the dirty dishes into the dishwasher and stared at Geoff. Closing his eyes, Ben dropped his head. God, he'd never even thought about Adam's funeral. He didn't even know where to begin with arranging one, let alone how he was going to pay it.

"I haven't....shit." What sort of friend was he to forget about Adam?

"His body's still at the morgue, but we can go ahead and arrange a funeral."

Gasping, Ben asked, "Has no one come forward to claim him?"

"Not from his family, no. From what I can gather, they located his family, but they didn't want anything to do with him. So, his body has been in the morgue. I've looked at costs, and it isn't cheap."

"Fuck! I don't know how I can pay for one. I don't have a job, and I'm living here for free." What the fuck was he supposed to do? He couldn't leave him there. He paced the kitchen floor, running his hand through his hair when Geoff stood in front of him, placing his hands on his shoulders, halting his pacing.

"I've spoken with Tom and Seb and we'll pay for it."

"What?" Ben shook his head. "No. No, you can't do that. You didn't even know him!"

"But you and Tom did. What kind of person would I be to leave it to you, Tom, and the others to sort it out, knowing what you've been through? Seb and I agree: we'll arrange it and pay for it. However, if you want to help out when you can, then that's fine. I know Tom is putting something towards it, and I also know Matt and Luke will try as well. Adam was lucky to have friends like you."

Geoff offering to pay was more than he had ever expected, and his eyes started to burn. He blinked rapidly to try and stop the tears from falling, but failed. Geoff pull him in and held him as he cried, rubbing his back. Ben was going to bury his friend. He was finally going to have the chance to say goodbye.

After a few minutes, he pulled back and Geoff handed him a tissue. Wiping his eyes and blowing his nose, Ben grimaced. Bet he looked good with snot on his face. "God, I'm sorry. I didn't mean to snot all over you."

Geoff chuckled. "No, it's fine. You okay with the funeral then?"

"Yes, yes, I am." Smiling, Ben leaned up and kissed Geoff. "I never thought about him being left there, and I feel a bit shit now. Still, I can't believe his family didn't want to know. He was their son! Why would they do that?" Ben asked Geoff, confused as to why Adam's family would behave the way they had. Their son was dead. Whatever had happened between them when he was alive could be forgiven now he was dead.

Shaking his head, Geoff frowned. "I don't know. Do you know why he was on the streets?"

"No. I know things weren't too good at home, but he never went into details. He could be kinda private like that, but he was a good friend, and he always had my back. I probably wouldn't be here if it weren't for him and then Tom."

"I'm glad they were there for you." Geoff reached up and palmed his face.

"I think I need a wash. My face kinda feels funny." Ben gave Geoff a wobbly smile. "I'll be back in a minute."

"No. Meet me in my bedroom," Geoff told him a firm voice, his face expressionless.

"Er, now?" Ben blinked at Geoff rapidly.

"Now."

Leaving the kitchen and sprinting upstairs, Ben washed quickly then slowly walked into Geoff's bedroom. It was definitely a man's room. The furniture was all dark woods, and the walls were an off-white colour. The carpet was cream and thick and Ben sank his feet into it, pausing when he saw Geoff stood by the bed.

"Are you sure about wanting a relationship with me?"

Now was the time to stop things before they went too far. Ben looked at Geoff. He wanted him. He'd wanted him for some time now.

He wanted more than the kisses they had shared. He nodded, walking over to where Geoff stood.

"Strip, then on your knees."

Ben fumbled as he tried to get his pants undone. His fingers didn't seem to want to cooperate. Stopping, Ben took a deep breath before trying again. Once he was naked, he knelt before Geoff. He closed his eyes, hoping Geoff wouldn't be repulsed by the scars that littered his body.

"Keep your head up but your eyes down. I don't want to see you with your head bowed."

Ben nodded and adjusted his position.

"Better. Good boy."

Ben felt that shiver across his skin again. He really liked being called a good boy. He listened to the sounds of Geoff footsteps as he walked around him and was very aware in that moment of his nakedness.

"Get up and lie on the bed, face up, legs spread."

Ben followed Geoff's instructions and lay down staring at the ceiling above the bed. He could hear clothing rustling, and next thing, Geoff was lying next to him naked.

"We'll start slow, so I can ease you into this."

"What? No sex?" Ben turned to look at him.

"We will have sex, but I'm not going to throw you into the deep end with this lifestyle. Slow and steady, that way you can gauge your likes and dislikes. We will have a contract, and you can read through all that this lifestyle entails."

"Like safe words?"

Smiling, Geoff nodded. "Yes. Safe words are very important. There are many aspects to the BDSM lifestyle."

Ben nodded. "Yes. I saw some of them on the websites you mentioned. Golden showers? Scat? Er no."

Geoff grimaced. "Not for me either. This is why we need to go over a checklist of sorts to find out our boundaries, what we are willing to try or are curious about trying. Then, there are the aspects that you don't ever want to try."

"So tonight?"

"I get to learn about you," Geoff muttered, leaning over Ben and kissing him.

Ben moaned into the kiss, opening his mouth, letting Geoff's tongue invade his mouth so their tongues danced together. He loved the way Geoff kissed him. Possessive. Dominant. Totally focused on him. Like he was the most important person in Geoff's world.

When Geoff moved to lie between his legs, Ben gasped. Geoff's hard cock rubbed against his own. It was the first time Ben had ever felt that before. He knew he was going to experience many firsts with Geoff.

Ben wallowed in the sensation. The heat and the sticky wetness as they rubbed together caused him to moan. Geoff kissed him like he owned him and Ben loved it. When Geoff broke the kiss, Ben panted, closing his eyes, arching up when Geoff kissed and licked his way down his neck.

The sting of Geoff biting his collarbone caused Ben to jerk beneath him, the slight pain making him shudder. Geoff moved down, biting Ben's nipple. Sucking it into his mouth, Geoff flicked it with his tongue, causing it to harden. Releasing it, Geoff blew across it and Ben moaned, feeling it harden more. Geoff moved to his other nipple and did the same to it as he twisted the one he'd already bitten. Ben lifted his hips up, rubbing against Geoff's stomach, leaving a damp trail there.

Geoff continued to kiss and lick his way down Ben's abdomen, paying particular attention to the scars along his hips. Ben closed his eyes as they prickled, the threat of tears close to the surface. Ben had never let anyone see them, let alone touch, kiss or lick them.

Geoff kissed his abdomen, murmuring, "Shh, Ben. It's alright."

Ben swallowed, nodding his head. He'd been afraid Geoff would stop wanting him once he'd seen his scars up close.

His eyes flew open when Geoff took the head of his dick into his mouth.

"Oh, God..."

Dropping his head back, Ben cried out. The sensation was overwhelming. Warm, moist, tight. He shuddered, his balls pulling up and Ben gritted his teeth against his impending orgasm. He didn't want to come. Not yet.

Geoff licked around the head before sucking on the head. Next thing Ben felt was Geoff taking him in down to the root. He cried out in pleasure, sensations flowing through his body. Ben couldn't stop thrusting his hips up, wanting more of that heat and wetness around him, and he felt Geoff hold him down as he continued to suck his cock.

Geoff alternated between deep throating him and licking and sucking the spongy head of his cock. He felt a wet finger circling his hole, gently pressing against it before circling around it again. Geoff's finger continued to do this, and then Ben bit back a moan when it eventually breached his muscle. The finger was gently moved in and out as Geoff continued to work his cock. He shot up from the bed when he felt Geoff touch that spot inside him and cried out as he came, squeezing his eyes shut, straining against Geoff's hold on him.

"Oh fuck....fuck..."

His body moved erratically and Ben lost all control over it. Pleasure swarmed through him and he cried out again as more ribbons of come pulsed from his dick.

When his body finally eased, Ben was panting. He opened his eyes to find Geoff staring down at him smiling before taking his mouth in a deep kiss. He could feel Geoff slip his finger out of his hole and he moaned slightly as the loss.

Geoff moved to Ben's side and pulled him close and Ben rested his head on Geoff's shoulder. His eyes started to grow heavy as Geoff stroked his back.

"Erm, that was the first time I've ever had someone, er, suck, er, you know," he told Geoff hesitantly, heat flooding his already flushed skin.

"And you enjoyed it?"

Ben blushed even more, nodding. Why the fuck was he blushing?

"I'm glad. Sleep now, Ben," Geoff whispered as Ben's eyes closed.

Chapter Twelve

Lying in bed watching Geoff dress, Ben sighed. Geoff had given him another explosive orgasm that morning. He'd come so many times over the last few weeks his balls were beginning to ache, but not once had Geoff tried to have sex with him. Geoff always paid attention to his scars, telling him that he was beautiful, that he was perfect.

It was all about Ben's enjoyment. Several times he'd tried to reciprocate, but Geoff had given him a smile and told him that he wanted Ben to enjoy this and not to worry about Geoff.

But, Ben did worry. He worried that Geoff didn't want to have sex with him because of what he'd done. Who would want to fuck an ex-hooker?

Later that morning, Ben met Tom for lunch and brought up what was happening between him and Geoff and his fears as to why Geoff wouldn't have sex with him.

"So, what do you think? Do you think it's because of what I used to do?"

Tom stared of into the distance for a minute then shook his head. "The first few times I was with Seb, he didn't fuck me, I fucked him. He wanted it that way so I would know it didn't bother him what I'd done previously. He wanted me to get as much pleasure from it as possible." Tom chuckled. "The next morning after our night together? Fuck, my balls ached and I swear Seb was limping."

Ben chuckled along with Tom. Whenever he saw the two of them together, it was obvious how much they loved one another. The way they would look at each other. The fact that they knew when the other was close. And their smiles. It was the type of smile you only gave that special person in your life.

"So, I should just give it more time?"

"It's been what, three weeks? If you want more, then you need to tell him. He could be waiting for you to let him know that you're ready for your relationship to move forward."

Ben tilted his head, thinking over what Tom had said. "When d'ya get so smart?"

Tom smiled looking over at him, but didn't say anything

"Seb's good for you. I can't remember ever seeing you this happy and relaxed. It's nice to see."

Tom looked away, but Ben caught the blush on Tom's cheeks and smiled to himself. He knew both Matt and Luke were doing well and had settled with Seb and Tom. He was grateful that they had all managed to escape the streets, but his chest always felt heavy because one of them hadn't made it.

He sighed thinking about Adam, but now he was coming to realise that maybe he couldn't have said or done anything to change him. Clara had helped him with that and writing in his journal.

He turned to Tom when he heard Tom scrunch up the bag that had held his sandwich. "Time to go?"

Tom nodded. "Lunchtime over. Can't be late either because I work for a right bastard."

"Fuck off." Ben laughed.

Tom stood and faced Ben. "Do what you feel is right. I'm here if you need to talk."

Ben nodded as they hugged and waved as Tom walked away. He sat and thought about how to approach the issue and when he had decided what he was going to do, he stood and quickly walked away.

❋ ❋ ❋

Geoff walked into the kitchen and frowned. The house seemed eerily quiet. He was used to coming in and seeing Ben or smelling something delicious cooking, but there was nothing.

"Ben?"

He paused, waiting for an answer, but none came. He quickly checked all the rooms before he went upstairs. He stopped suddenly at the threshold of his bedroom and took in the sight before him. Ben lying naked on his bed. Blindfolded. Condoms and lube on his chest. Cock hard and leaking.

Geoff arched an eyebrow, tilting his head to the side and took his time looking over Ben. It was easy to observe Ben's nervousness. His chest moved quickly in time with his breaths and he would clench his fists before releasing them. One of Ben's feet moved continuously from side to side barely pausing.

He walked into the en-suite and stripped before taking one of the

New Beginnings

quickest showers ever. Drying off, he walked back into the bedroom and found Ben in the same position he had left him in. He dropped the towel on the floor and crawled up the bed to hover over Ben as he moved the condom and lube from Ben's chest and onto the bed beside them.

"Are you trying to tell me something?" He didn't try to keep the amusement out of his voice.

He watched Ben take a shuddery breath in and then swallow. "I'm sorry, it's just I really want you to fuck me."

Geoff lowered his body onto Ben's, pushing the blindfold up. He watched Ben blink a few times, his eyes adjusting to the light before he bent to kiss him, plunging his tongue into Ben's mouth, swallowing his moan.

Their tongues danced and Geoff groaned when Ben's hard, leaking cock rubbed on his hip as Ben arched up.

Breaking off from the kiss, Geoff moved down Ben's body and gripped Ben's cock. He looked into Ben's eyes, seeing the lust on his face, and lowered his mouth onto its head, sucking hard. Ben moaned as his hips came off the bed, forcing more of his cock into Geoff's mouth. Geoff moaned around the head and heard Ben's answering groan above him.

He blindly searched around the bed until he found the lube, and opened the cap to pour some on his fingers. He wouldn't go slow tonight. He'd been aching for weeks, wanting to sink into Ben's hole, but didn't want to rush him. Geoff wanted Ben to come to him. And Ben had.

Making sure his fingers were covered, he spread Ben's legs, and moved between them as he began to trace his hole with his finger, feeling the muscle flutter beneath it.

He felt Ben's cock twitch in his mouth as he slowly pushed his finger in passed the ring of muscle. Geoff held it there for a few seconds until Ben whimpered and then he started to move it slowly in and out. Ben groaned again and Geoff could feel him trying to get more of his finger in his arse.

Pulling his finger out, he pushed two back in and moved them around until he heard Ben cry out above him and arch off the bed as he suddenly came. Geoff swallowed it all and when Ben finally slumped back onto the bed, Geoff pulled his fingers free and reached for the condom. He opened it and rolled it on and then squirted lube on his cock, making sure it was completely covered, then lay back down between Ben's legs. Ben looked up into his eyes as Geoff rubbed his cock up and down Ben's crease, teasing him about what was to come.

Ben bit his lip, moving his arse, trying to get Geoff to push his dick into his hole.

"Please," Ben whimpered above him.

Geoff caught Ben's gaze and held it as he slowly pushed in. He groaned when the head slipped past Ben's muscle and he heard Ben gasp above him. He froze, muscles tense as he held himself still. Geoff had to wait for Ben to adjust.

When Ben finally nodded at Geoff, he pushed in slowly until he felt his balls against Ben's arse. Geoff groaned when he was fully in, closing his eyes, gripping the sheets in his hands. The heat and tightness was almost enough to make him come, but he wanted this to last for Ben. He wanted Ben to understand that their first time together was going to be nothing like he'd experienced on the streets. He held still, waiting for Ben to tell him it was alright to move.

"Please tell me I can move," Geoff eventually groaned out.

Swallowing, Ben nodded his head. "Yeah, I'm good."

Geoff moved in and out with shallow strokes, never too fast or hard. With each stroke, Geoff moved slightly until he heard Ben gasp and cry out. He'd found Ben's hot spot.

Making sure he hit it every time, Geoff bent down to kiss Ben, pulling him into his arms and holding him tight. Ben's legs wrapped around Geoff's back and he moved a hand down to grip Ben's arse, tilting it up so he could go deeper. Geoff moaned at the smooth slide of skin against skin, feeling the sweat coating their bodies aid the movement, allowing them to glide against one another.

It wasn't long before Geoff moved faster, harder into Ben. Ben encouraged him, his feet pushing on Geoff's arse, pulling him in.

"Please....harder..." Ben gasped.

Geoff reared up and grabbed Ben's legs, moving them over his arms before he grabbed Ben's cock and started stroking him in time with his thrusts. Ben's back arched off the bed, crying out as Geoff pounded into him.

Geoff watched Ben arch off the bed again, shouting, his body jerking. Ben's dick in his hand swelled then jerked, ropes of come shooting from the head. Geoff's hand was covered in warm, wet come and Ben's arse tightened around his cock. Geoff continued to stroke Ben through his orgasm as his own balls pulled up. A tingling sensation started in Geoff's balls and soon moved up his shaft and pulsed along his hole.

Geoff's orgasm hit, causing him to jerk erratically, legs trembling as ribbons of come shot from his dick. Geoff lost control of his body, his orgasm flowing over him.

When it finally eased, he dropped Ben's legs and collapsed on top of him, panting hard, his head on Ben's neck. He felt Ben's arms come around him and hold him tight and he lifted his head to kiss Ben gently on the lips. He continued to kiss Ben slowly, waiting for his breathing and heart rate to return to normal.

When his dick softened, Geoff leaned back and carefully pulled out, both moaning slightly at the sensation. He removed the condom and tied it off before throwing it in the bin next to the bed. He lay next to Ben and stroked the wet hair from Ben's forehead, smiling at him.

Taking in Ben's flushed face and chest, Geoff asked, "Are you alright?"

"Yeah." Ben tilted his head, smiling at Geoff.

"Everything was good for you?"

"Yeah."

Geoff laughed quietly. "Good. I wanted to make sure you enjoyed it as much as I did."

Biting his lip and lowering his gaze, Ben asked, "I was okay, then?"

Geoff heard the tremor in Ben's voice so grabbed his hand and placed it on his hardening cock. "What do you think?" he asked him, cocking his eyebrow.

Ben blushed, looking away, and Geoff chuckled. He stood and pulled Ben up from the bed. "Take away?"

"God, yes. I don't want to cook now," Ben told him as he stretched and then winced slightly.

"Sore?"

"Not too much actually."

Geoff leaned over him and kissed him. "Good. Let's get some clothes on and order some food."

Within thirty minutes, they were sat in the living room eating a curry and watching some documentary on the African Plains. Once they'd finished, Geoff took Ben's hand and led him back to the bedroom. Once was not going to be enough tonight.

New Beginnings

※ ※ ※

Geoff woke to find Ben snuggled into his side, arm around his chest and a leg thrown over his hip. He chuckled to himself. It was like being wrapped up by an octopus. He slowly untangled himself and climbed out of the bed then walked to the bathroom to have a shower. He was due in court today in a fraud case that had taken almost two years to complete. He wanted to get there early to ensure he had all the relevant details before going to court.

When Geoff had finished in the shower, he ran a bath for Ben. He'd fucked him hard, and he knew Ben would be a little sore this morning, so a bath would help ease him. He walked back into his room and started to get dressed while looking over at the man sleeping in his bed. Yes, he was over ten years older than him, but Ben had lived a hard life and in some ways it had matured him, but in others, he still held an innocence that appealed to Geoff.

He loved the unique colour of his eyes. How one minute they looked green then another minute they would look blue. Ben's dark brown hair lay over his face, obscuring some of it from view. But it was those dimples that flashed whenever he smiled that always caught Geoff's eyes and made him pause for breath. The man was beautiful. How anyone could have mistreated him as a child was a mystery to him, and he hoped his parents had a long, miserable life.

He checked the temperature of the bath before walking over to the bed and sitting on the side next to Ben. He reached over and gently moved Ben's hair off his face, letting the strands slip through his fingers before leaning down and kissing him on his forehead. He watched Ben stir then slowly open his beautiful eyes to look up at him.

"Morning. I've run you a bath. Thought you might need it."

He watched Ben move closer to him, wincing slightly before

looking at him and blushing.

"Yeah, I'm a bit sore."

"Sorry." He leaned down again, kissing him on the lips. "Get in the bath and I'll bring you up a coffee."

Leaving Ben in the bedroom, Geoff went into the kitchen and poured a mug for Ben. When Geoff returned, he found him in the bath groaning.

"God, that feels good," Ben murmured, leaning back in the tub.

Placing the mug on the edge of the bath, Geoff told Ben, "I'm in court today, so you won't be able to reach me, but I'll see you tonight."

Ben nodded with his eyes closed. "Good luck," he mumbled.

Geoff chuckled, kissing him before getting up to leave. He left a copy of the contract in the kitchen with a note telling Ben to read through it and that they would talk when he got back. Yes, he'd done things back to front. He should have given Ben the contract sooner, but he hadn't been entirely certain that they would reach this stage.

Grabbing his briefcase, he quickly checked the contents before getting his coat, wallet and keys and leaving the house.

Chapter Thirteen

When he arrived at the office, Geoff found Seb already in, collecting some files and putting them in his bag. Seb was attending court with him today, so he wasn't surprised to see him there.

"Ready?" Geoff asked him.

"Yes. Just doing some last minute checks," he muttered, frowning.

"Me too. Let's go before it gets busy."

They walked out of the office and made their way onto the street. The pavements were starting to get crowded, and the traffic was bumper to bumper, which made him grateful for the early start he'd planned.

Outside the courts stood his client, James Flynn, pacing as he waited for them, chewing his nails. When he spotted them, he virtually sprinted over. "Are you sure we're going to win?"

Geoff shook James' hand before assuring him. "Yes. We have all the evidence. There isn't any plausible defence he can mount. The trail shows he siphoned money from you for at least three years. Things will be fine, and you know Seb has put in the hours to trace every last penny."

James' shoulders slumped slightly and he exhaled deeply. "How long will it last?"

"That I can't answer. Could be a couple of days or a couple of weeks. We won't really know until we're in there and get started. Let's go, shall we?"

It was a long day, and as it progressed, Geoff began to realise that he might be here for a few days. The man's defence was that he had needed the money for his sick wife. Geoff couldn't help but feel sorry for the man and what his family had gone through, but he had stolen money from his employer and should be held accountable for that. He was clearly trying to earn some sympathy from the jury. He sighed. He could see how this week was going to go.

※ ※ ※

When Geoff drove home, he had a pounding headache behind his eyes. He literally winced every time he turned his head too quickly. He parked his car and walked into his house. The wonderful aroma hit him, and he groaned. He was hungry, but first he desperately needed some painkillers.

Walking into the kitchen, Geoff stopped to watch Ben move around dishing out the food. He enjoyed coming home to this. Not the meal waiting for him part, though he did like that, but the fact that someone was here with him. He hadn't realised how lonely he was until Ben had moved in, and he could admit to himself that he didn't want Ben to leave.

Frowning. Geoff attempted to analyse his feelings, but eventually gave up as the pounding in his head worsened. It felt like a brass band was playing in there now.

"Hi."

Ben turned and smiled at him, dimples popping out, then walked over to him, kissing him lightly on the lips. "How was your day in court?"

"Long and tiring."

"Hmmm, you look a little pale. Are you feeling alright?" Ben frowned, looking at his face.

"Headache," Geoff admitted, "but I've got some painkillers in the cupboard, so I'll take some then get changed. What have you been doing today?"

"My exam results came, so I've been looking at courses."

"That's great! So..." Geoff grinned at him, waiting for Ben to tell him how he'd done.

"Well, A's." Ben smiled shyly at him as he told him.

"A's? I don't think I got straight A's when I took my exams! Have you decided then?"

"I always loved science. How things work, so I'm going to do that."

"What? Chemistry, biology and physics?"

"And maths."

"Shit! Really? That's a lot. Going to keep you busy."

"Do you think it's too much?" Ben asked, eyebrows drawn together and biting his lip.

Reaching out, Geoff pulled Ben's lip from between his teeth. "If anyone can do it, you can. You're very intelligent, and these results prove that."

Ben ducked his head, and Geoff had to smile. It was nice to see the real Ben come out after what he had been like when he first moved in. He moved over to him, tilting his face up so he could kiss him. What was meant to be a quick kiss turned into more as their tongues moved together. When Ben moaned, Geoff picked him up and sat him on the counter, pulling his shirt off. Ben leaned back as Geoff kissed his way down his chest. He felt Ben's hands grab his hair as he undid the button of his jeans.

"Up."

Ben lifted his hips up, and Geoff pulled his jeans and boxers down low enough so he could get to his cock. He licked around the head, sliding his tongue into the slit before swallowing him down whole.

"Geoff, oh fuck. That feels so good!"

He bobbed up and down keeping a strong seal around Ben's dick as Ben's hand grabbed his hair tightly. He wanted to get him off. Within a couple of minutes, he heard Ben cry out.

"Coming, Geoff, oh...."

His mouth filled with Ben's come, and he swallowed it all; he didn't want to waste a drop. When Ben had finished coming, Geoff slowly let his soft cock slip from his lips and reached to grab Ben by his hair, kissing him forcefully, thrusting his tongue into Ben's mouth, moaning. He loved the taste of Ben. He slowed the kiss until they were exchanging small touches, and eventually he pulled away.

"Congrats, Ben," he smiled at Ben.

Ben looked at him dazed but satiated, then gave him a wide smile, dimples on show. "Wow. I'm looking forward to more exam results in the future."

Geoff smirked at him then helped him get off the counter and dressed.

"Can I smell lamb?"

"Yes. I'm doing a roast. I've missed them, and after getting those results, I thought I'd cook one tonight."

"Sit down and I'll finish it off. What's left?"

"Nothing much now. The lamb's resting, the roast potatoes are almost done, and the veg is ready. Just carve the meat and I'll set the table."

"Alright."

Once everything was ready, they sat down to eat. Geoff moaned when he tasted the lamb. Cooked just how he liked it. It wasn't long before Geoff had cleared his plate and sat back in his chair relaxing.

"I read the contract." Ben looked at him from under his lashes.

"And?"

"I've filled it in. Er, what I would like, what I might try and some definite nos."

"Do you have it here? I'd like to have a look at it."

Ben stood, walked over to one of the drawers in the kitchen, and pulled the contract out before walking back and handing it over.

Geoff scanned the sections and an idea formed in his mind.

He dropped the contract on the counter, then grabbed Ben's hand leading him to his bedroom.

"Strip and drop."

Ben stared at him blankly for a few seconds then drew in a shuddering breath before undressing. Geoff could see how turned on he was. His cock was hard and leaking. He watched Ben lower himself into a kneeling position in front of him.

"Tonight, I'm going to handcuff you, then have you ride me. Are you comfortable with that?"

Ben hesitated before answering his question. "Yes."

"Are you sure? You've marked it as something you want to try, but I don't want to rush you."

Ben smiled slightly at him. "I'm nervous, but I want to try this."

Geoff nodded. "Alright. What are your safe words?"

"Er, no?"

Geoff shook his head as he answered him. "Can't be the word no. Sometimes people say no when they mean yes, so a safe word is always a different word you wouldn't use in sex. How about colours for now. Green is for okay, amber for when you want to slow down and red is when you want it to stop."

Ben nodded. "Yeah, alright."

"But you need to think of a safe word that's relevant for you. Now, on the bed on your front with your hands above your head."

He watched Ben assume the position he'd wanted. Unable to resist touching him, Geoff ran his hands along his skin. He noticed the faded scars, but they didn't bother Geoff. Ben had survived a terrible childhood and Geoff would ensure Ben only knew pleasure from now on.

Moving away from Ben's tempting body, Geoff reached into the drawer and pulled out a set of padded handcuffs. Leaning over, he put them on Ben. "Not too tight?"

Ben tested them. "No."

"The answer is no, Sir."

"Huh?"

"In here when we are doing a scene you will call me Sir. Clear?"

When Ben didn't answer, Geoff knelt by the bed and turned Ben's head towards him. His eyes were closed, and he was panting slightly. "Colour?" he asked him quietly.

Ben shuddered then swallowed, licking his lips before he answered. "Green. Fuck, we are so green."

Geoff rocked back on his heels, eyes wide open in surprise. He'd expected Ben to be apprehensive, but he appeared even more turned on. He bent and kissed him then stood up and took the tube of lube out of the drawer.

"Hands and knees." Geoff ordered in a firm, low voice.

After Ben had moved into the position Geoff wanted, not easy with the handcuffs on, Geoff knelt behind him and spread his arse cheeks open, exposing his hole. Rubbing his finger over it, Geoff watched the wrinkled flesh tighten then relax. Teasing it, Geoff pressed against it, but never penetrated Ben's hole.

Leaning closer, Geoff flicked his tongue over Ben's hole and moaned at the taste. Musky, all male. Uniquely Ben. He circled Ben's hole with his tongue slowly rimming him, feeling it clench beneath him. Moving away, Geoff licked down to his balls and then back up again, getting it all nice and wet.

Circling Ben's hole with his tongue, Geoff listened to the moans Ben made. The whimpers, the muttering and gasps of pleasure. The way Ben's body moved, pushing back on his tongue, shuddering beneath his hands. He'd never been into rimming, but with Ben, he wanted to explore that and so much more. He stiffened his tongue and then thrust it into Ben's hole, hearing Ben cry out. He heard the handcuffs rattle as Ben tugged on them, unable to control his body.

Geoff pulled back and told him, "You can't come until I tell you to."

"Yes, Sir," Ben shuddered, breathing hard, hands clenched.

Thrusting his tongue in again, Geoff swirled it around before pulling it out then fucked Ben with it. He added a finger and pushed his tongue in again continuing to fuck Ben with both. Geoff could feel Ben's body shiver and jerk with every thrust of his tongue and he added another finger, relaxing the muscle and widening him. He scissored his fingers and moved them around until he found Ben's prostate, rubbing against it. Ben cried out above him, body trembling.

"Please, can I come, Sir?" Ben asked him panting, arse clenching on Geoff's fingers in a vice-like grip.

Reaching a hand around Ben, Geoff gripped his cock, stroking it. Geoff leaned back down and resumed thrusting his tongue in Ben's arse. "Come," he ordered him.

Within seconds, Ben shouted out as he started to come, and Geoff could feel him clamping down on his fingers. Ben's body shuddered and jerked, come spurting from his dick to cover Geoff's hand and the covers below.

Geoff stroked a hand down Ben's sweat-covered back, feeling tremors run through Ben's body as his orgasm began to subside. Helping Ben to lie down on the bed, Geoff lay next to him, listening to Ben panting.

As Ben eventually calmed, Geoff stroked Ben's sweat-soaked hair from his forehead. "You did well, Ben. I'm proud of you."

Ben opened his eyes, looking at him in a daze. "I did?"

"Yes." Geoff leaned closer, sliding his lips over Ben's. He felt Ben sigh against them and Geoff pushed his tongue between Ben's lips. Ben opened his mouth and their tongues slowly slid past one another, touching and twirling in an erotic dance.

A minute later, Geoff pulled back. "Time to ride me now. I want to hear you cry my name as you ride my cock."

Ben moaned, closing his eyes. Pushing himself up, Geoff moved himself beneath Ben. He reached over, grabbed a condom, and opened it, rolling it on his hard dick, then added lube. He helped Ben to straddle him, then stopped moving. Geoff had never seen a more stunning sight. Ben's cheeks were flushed from his orgasm, his kiss swollen lips slightly parted, his sweaty hair sticking to his face, and his eyes half closed. Beautiful. Ben was beautiful.

He held his cock up for Ben and bit his lip watching Ben slowly lower himself onto it. Geoff groaned when the head of his dick pushed past the ring of muscle, the heat and tightness ramping up his own arousal. He knew he wouldn't last long, but as long as he was able to get Ben off again, he didn't mind. He watched Ben pull back up then drop further down on his cock. God, he was about to explode. Ben's movements were slow and torturous.

The look on Ben's face told Geoff exactly how much he was enjoying this. His head was thrown back, mouth open wide, his chest moving quickly as he panted. Ben kept repeating the action until he was fully seated on Geoff's cock, then he slowly dropped his head forward to look down at him.

"Ride me," Geoff ordered him. He didn't know how much longer he was going to last. He reached for Ben's cock and started stroking him as Ben slowly rode him, staring down and moaning every time he moved. It wasn't long before Ben was riding him hard and fast, crying out every time he dropped down. Geoff felt the tingling along his spine that signalled his impending orgasm and stroked Ben faster, gripping him tighter as Geoff's balls pulled up.

Ben suddenly clamped around him, shouting out as ribbons of

come coated Geoff's stomach and chest, moving erratically above him. Geoff continued stroking him through his orgasm when his own hit.

Thrusting up, Geoff cried out, grabbing Ben by his hips as he slammed up into his body, jerking as he filled the condom. Geoff's body flushed with heat, electricity shooting throughout as he continued coming.

Eventually, he lay back on the bed, Ben slumped over him, gasping for breath. That has to be one of those most intense orgasms he had ever had. What was it about Ben that made him feel this way?

He gently brushed the hair from Ben's forehead as their breathing slowly returned to normal then he eased Ben off him and removed the condom, throwing it in the bin. He leaned over and, grabbing the key, released the cuffs from Ben's wrists, rubbing them as he did. Ben opened his eyes, smiling up at him.

Grabbing some wipes, Geoff cleaned Ben then pulled him close. Ben reached a hand up and curled it around the back of Geoff's head, pulling him down for a slow, gentle kiss before closing his eyes. Geoff pulled the covers over them and watched as Ben fell asleep. Watching him sleep, Geoff realised he was falling for him, and that scared the shit out of him. He wasn't sure it was something he was ready for.

New Beginnings

Chapter Fourteen

Ben groaned as he sat reading through funeral plans and looking at the costs. How could a wooden box cost *so* much? No wonder it was a booming business. There were church costs, hearses, flowers, tombstone and much more. It could cost from three grand to over ten! Burying someone was more expensive than he'd realised. He didn't know about church services and hymns or types of flowers. He dropped his head onto the counter, closing his eyes. He'd been at this all week and still didn't have anything set in place.

Fortunately, everyone was coming over for dinner, so the four of them could sit together and go over the various plans available and start the whole process rolling. The thought of Adam lying in the dark on a cold metal slab left a cold, hollow feeling in Ben's chest. He hated the thought of him being there alone, which he knew was stupid. He was dead, so he wasn't feeling anything. But Ben knew and he hated it.

He pushed away from the counter and poured himself a coffee. As he sipped it, the phone rang. He put the mug down and walked over to pick it up.

"Hello."

"Hey, Ben, it's Luke."

Ben smiled. "Hey, you alright?"

"Are we still on for later?"

"Yeah. Six alright for you guys?" Ben opened the fridge, checking if he needed any ingredients.

"Yeah, we'll meet you there. I know Tom and Seb are going straight from work."

"It's great that Tom has a job, isn't it?" Ben was happy for Tom, and from what Geoff had told him, Tom was fitting in well. "How about you? What are you doing?"

"Both me and Matt are working and we're both going to college."

Ben laughed. "That's great! I might be joining you. I'm thinking of doing science and maths."

"Holy shit!" Luke gasped. "I'm doing English Lit and business."

"What about Matt? Has he decided what he's doing?"

"Yeah, languages."

Ben paused. "Really? I didn't know he could speak any."

"Yeah, he did French and German at school. He just picks it up. I've always been jealous about how quickly he could learn it, when I was still trying to say 'hello.'"

"I know Tom's going back as well."

"Yeah, he never finished, did he? He never got that chance. At least we'll all be going the same place, so we'll know each other."

"I'm looking forward to it." Ben couldn't wait to go back.

"Me too, but I'm a little scared, you know. It's been a while and what do I say to people when they ask me what I've been doing? I can hardly say selling sex." Ben heard Luke sigh. He had a point.

"We'll think of something before we start." What would they say? "Anyway, I've got to go. I'm cooking tonight."

"Want us to bring anything?"

"Nah, I've got it covered, but thanks for offering. See you guys later."

"Bye."

Ben put the phone down and stood staring at it. He hadn't even thought about the people he would meet. Luke was right. What would he talk about? What could he say about his past? He chewed his thumbnail when he thought about it. Shit! Was he doing the right thing by going to college? He ran his hand through his hair, his stomach twisted in nerves, and his hands were suddenly clammy. He put his hand on his chest; his heart was racing, and he wasn't even at college yet.

Could he do it? He knew he wanted to continue his education now he had the chance, but he didn't want everyone to know what he'd done to survive. He didn't want them to look at him that way, like he was dirty or scum. He wasn't ashamed exactly; he'd done what he'd had to do to survive. He would probably be dead if he hadn't.

What family he did have had treated him like shit and the only person who had cared for him had died. So he'd been on his own with no food, money, and nowhere to live, and he'd made friends, people who'd done the same things he had done to survive. They understood. Maybe he should talk to them later.

Looking at the clock, he realised he needed to start getting the food ready for dinner. There would be six in total tonight, and he wanted to make sure he had plenty in. Checking the fridge again and the cupboards, he made a list of ingredients he needed and went to the supermarket. An hour later, he was back and started to prep. He was going with Italian as he knew Geoff loved it. Italian garlic chicken with ham, basil and beans.

Once everything was prepped and the chicken was in the oven, Ben showered and changed into clean clothes. He went about cleaning the place up and making sure they had plenty of beer and wine. He checked the chicken to see how far along it was, and when he closed the oven, was surprised to see Geoff stood watching him, causing him to jump in surprise.

He put his hand on his chest, "God, you made me jump. I wasn't expecting you until later."

"Sorry. The case finished, so I decided to come home early."

"Did it go your way?"

Geoff nodded as he walked over to the oven and peeked inside. "I'm glad it's over. James, our client, is ecstatic that it's all finished. It's been draining for him having this hanging over his head." Geoff inhaled. "Smells wonderful. What is it?"

"Italian garlic chicken. Are you in for the night now?"

"Yes. I've got a couple of bits to finish in the study, and that's me for the weekend. Did you get the suit for tomorrow?"

Damn, he was hoping Geoff had forgotten that he'd asked him. He had some work function at a posh hotel and had invited Ben, which Ben didn't want to go to, but he felt like he couldn't turn down the invite. He knew it was important to Geoff and considering what was happening between them-- something he still couldn't quite put a name to-- he'd agreed to go. He wouldn't know anyone there and was probably going to be the youngest person, so he was bound to stick out. Also, what would he talk about? He knew nothing about Geoff's job or what type of cases he dealt with. Maybe he should ask him about it. Learn a bit so he wouldn't look like a complete idiot and end up embarrassing Geoff.

Geoff must have seen some of the unease of Ben's face. "Are you alright going tomorrow?"

Ben shrugged as he answered, "I'm nervous. I'm not gonna know anyone, and I don't know what you do, not really. I just don't want to make you look silly. Who am I? What will you tell people about me?"

Geoff pulled Ben close, looking into his eyes. "You won't make me look silly. There will be plenty of people there who don't know everything about what their partners do. It's not like we can talk about the details of the cases we deal with, so don't worry about that. As for who you are? I'll introduce you as my partner because that's who you are, and you're going to college. I'm proud of who you are and who you're becoming. This--" he pointed between them-- "isn't some casual fling. I don't do them. If you don't want serious relationship with me, you need to tell me now before this continues." Geoff paused, then asked, "Am I who *you* want?"

Ben stared at Geoff, thinking about the question he'd asked him. Was Geoff who he wanted? Was this what he wanted? Or was he doing this because he was grateful that someone had helped him get his shit together and was giving him the chance to live a normal life and get off the streets? He chewed his bottom lip thinking about the answers to those questions. He liked Geoff, really liked him. Ben had strong feelings for him. He probably loved him, but Ben wasn't ready to look into that just yet. Geoff made him laugh, made him feel important. He didn't hold him back. Geoff wanted him to pursue his dreams, whatever they were. And the best thing? Geoff never expected sex from Ben. Yeah, he wanted this.

"I want this with you. I was worried at one point that you wouldn't let me stay if I didn't have sex with you, but you've never made me feel like I had to."

Clenching his jaw, Geoff told him, "I would never, *never* expect you to sleep with me so that you could stay here."

"I know that now, but at first I wasn't so sure. You don't hold me back, you know. You want me to do things with my life, and you've never asked for anything in return. You've never forced yourself on me. You left that up to me to decide. Man, I got naked and knelt on the floor for you and you didn't ask for that!" Ben shrugged. Thinking about that day embarrassed him and he felt the heat on his throat and cheeks, but it had gotten the result he'd wanted.

"You were so hot, knelt on the floor, waiting for me."

Ben smiled shyly at Geoff, looking at him from under his hair. "Really?"

"Really, but I don't want to talk about that as we have friends coming in less than an hour and answering the door with a hard on? No." Geoff laughed.

Ben stepped towards Geoff, sighing against his chest. He lifted his head, kissing him before pulling away. "Go, get ready. I still have some things to finish up here."

"Alright. Did you look at the funeral details?"

Ben growled, pushing away and stomping over to the plans. He picked them up and waved them at Geoff before throwing that back on the side. "Yes, and I still don't know what to do. I've been tearing my hair out going over the details. Thank God the guys are coming over, so they can help me sort this out."

Geoff walked over to him kissing him again, then walked towards the stairs. "I'll get changed and come down to help. It'll get easier, I promise."

New Beginnings

Ben continued getting everything set up for dinner. When Geoff came in, Ben stopped what he was doing and drooled. He was only wearing a white shirt and faded blue jeans, but damn, he looked hot!

Geoff sauntered over to Ben, lifting his face up. "You like?"

Ben nodded dumbly. Oh, he liked alright.

Geoff kissed him, and Ben whimpered when Geoff's tongue trace his lips. He opened his mouth, feeling Geoff suck on his tongue. He put his arms around Geoff's neck, entwining his fingers in his hair and felt his arse being grabbed and then he was lifted up, flush against Geoff's body, their erections rubbing together. The friction was amazing. He moaned, rubbing against Geoff, attacking his mouth and wrapping his legs around him. It was such a turn on, knowing Geoff could pick him up with ease.

Geoff licked and nibbled down Ben's neck when the doorbell rang. Groaning in frustration, Ben dropped his head onto Geoff's shoulder, taking some deep breaths as Geoff lowered him to the floor.

Ben chuckled, looking at him. "Someone's early, cock blockers!"

Geoff laughed out loud, looking at Ben. "Damn right."

Ben watched Geoff attempt to rearrange his hard on before he walked out to answer the door. He walked back in less than a minute later with Seb and Tom behind him.

"Drink?" Geoff asked them as they went to the fridge.

"God yes. Beers please," Seb answered. "I've never been so happy for a case to be over. I felt for Mr Flynn. He's been through enough and then a court case on top. It should never have gotten that far."

The doorbell went again as Geoff passed a couple of bottles over to Seb. "That should be Matt and Luke."

As Geoff answered the door, Tom asked Ben, "How're ya doing?"

"Alright. Being here with Geoff has helped. I've decided on what courses I want to do, and I've completed all the forms so I should be starting in September. What about you? Looking forward to going back?"

Tom looked uncertain. "Yes and no. I left almost five years ago now, so it might take some getting used to, but I want a decent job, so I need an education."

"Any ideas what you want to do?"

"Yeah. I guess working with Seb has let me see what goes on there, and I like it. I know I'm only doing the filing, but Geoff's showed me some stuff as well. I enjoy it." Tom shrugged.

"Wow, a solicitor." Ben thought about it. He could see Tom doing it. "It suits you."

"Really?" Tom glanced at him, biting his lip and peeling the label from his bottle of beer.

Ben reached over and stopped Tom as he smiled at him. "Yeah. No matter what happened, you kept things going for us. I don't think we'd be here if it weren't for you."

Tom frowned. "Adam isn't."

"I know. I spoke to Clara about it, and I think looking back on it, Adam wanted to go. He was using, which he hid from us, and he was taking more risks. I don't think we'll ever know for sure, will we. I still feel guilty about it. Not like I used to, but it's still there. He was my friend, and I miss him."

"Me too. Sometimes I see something, and I think 'oh, Adam would like that,' and it reminds me that he isn't here."

"Yeah, I know that feeling. Speak to Clara, Tom. It's helping me, and I never thought I'd say that."

"So it really is helping you, Ben?" Seb asked him.

Ben nodded, looking at Seb. "Yeah, it really is. It's hard at first to talk about what we went through, but it's helping me move on."

Ben watched Seb nudge Tom and give him a pointed look. Tom gave a dramatic sigh. "Okay, I get it. I'm not sure I can yet."

"Do a journal," Ben suggested. It helped him; maybe it would do the same for Tom.

"A journal? Oh, yeah, I forgot that Geoff had mentioned it," Seb told him.

"Write a journal. I found it helped me to write the things that I'd been through down in a journal. I wasn't ready to talk about what had happened to me, and I knew no one else would see it unless I wanted them to. It helped me face things."

"Why don't you try that, Tom?"

Tom looked between the two of them, the indecision evident on his face. He finally nodded. "Okay, okay. I'll try it."

"Sorry to butt in, but me and Luke have been talking, and we've decided to see someone too. We've seen how much it's helped Ben, so we thought we'd give it a try," Matt added.

"So, it's just me then, not going," Tom grumbled.

"You were on the streets longer than us, Tom," Matt spoke. "You've seen more and experienced more than us. It might be harder for you."

Seb put his arms around Tom's waist, pulling him back against his chest. Ben smiled at them as he went to get the chicken and heard Seb say to Tom, "Do what you feel is best for you. You know how I feel about this, but I'll support any decision you make."

"You will?"

"You know I will."

Geoff held up some bottles of beer. "Beers?"

Chapter Fifteen

Dinner was a success and, between them, they'd managed to arrange a funeral plan for Adam. Geoff sat with Seb talking quietly as he watched Ben with Tom, Matt and Luke as they decided on the details. It still surprised him how much Ben was changing. Gone was the angry, near silent boy and now he could see the beginnings of what he knew would be a confident man.

"I still can't believe how much it costs for a coffin. It's a piece of wood, for fuck's sake!" Tom threw his pen on the counter. "The person is dead and these companies are trying to get every last fuckin' penny they can."

"I know! I never knew it could cost this much," Luke agreed with him, rubbing his head with his hand.

"It doesn't matter. We've discussed this. Get him what you think he'd have liked and we'll sort out the cost at a later date," Geoff interrupted.

Ben had told him how Tom felt about it and in a way he could understand. It was expensive, but Adam was their friend, and he knew that they wanted the best for him. Adam hadn't had a great life, so now he was dead, they were going to give him a great send off.

"You're gonna let us help, right?" Matt asked him, glancing up from the brochure in front of him.

"Yes, you know I will. We'll work that out later." Geoff gave them a small smile. "Any closer to what you want?"

"Yeah." Ben stood up and yawned as he stretched. "We have the list here. You've sorted out everything with the police, right?"

"Don't worry about it. I've dealt with it. Now, let's have that list and tomorrow I can book everything."

"We need to head home as well. Thanks for inviting us, Geoff." Seb stood and walked over to Tom, pulling him up. "You two want a lift home?"

"Yeah, thanks." Luke said as he too stood up.

"Yes, I do. Come on. See you Monday, Geoff. Oh, and have a good time tomorrow." Facing Ben, Seb said, "Thanks for that, Ben."

"For what?" Ben asked frowning slightly.

"It might have been me going, so I owe you one."

"Great, just great," Ben mumbled.

"I heard that," Geoff whispered in Ben's ear.

"You were meant to."

Geoff walked them out and waved as they drove away. He locked up and found Ben sat in the kitchen staring at the counter. He stood behind him, pulling him to his chest, resting his chin on the top of Ben's head.

"You alright?" he asked him.

"Thinking about Adam and the funeral." He told him, giving him a small smile.

Geoff held him tightly for a minute. "Let's go to bed and relax. We've a long day tomorrow."

Ben stood, and Geoff held his hand leading him to his bedroom. Ben paused at the threshold, and Geoff looked at him searchingly before pulling him gently into the room.

"I wasn't sure..." Ben mumbled as he looked at the floor.

"You know I want you in my bed."

Ben shrugged and looked away. "We've had sex."

"I'm not like them, Ben. I thought you knew this."

"It's just sometimes it's hard to believe you'd want to be with me given everything I've done." Ben's shoulder slumped as he spoke.

"Have I ever made you feel that way?" Facing Ben, Geoff placed his hands on Ben's shoulders, rubbing gently.

"No, you haven't. I'm sorry."

"Don't apologise. Remember what Clara said? She said you would have days like this."

"Yeah."

"From now on, you sleep in here with me. I want you to."

He watched Ben blow out a breath. "I think discussing the funeral and talking about Adam raked everything up for me. All those insecurities." Ben stared into his eyes. "I want this with you. I wish I wasn't so fucked up."

"You've been through a lot. And it's going to take time." Geoff opened the walk-in wardrobe. "See, I've cleared a space for you. Move your things in tomorrow."

Ben gave him the biggest smile he'd ever seen, then grabbed his face and mashed their lips together. Geoff held his hips and manoeuvred them to the bed.

"How do you want me, Sir?"

Geoff shivered. He loved it when Ben called him Sir. "Strip. On your knees on the bed and hold the bed frame." He watched Ben follow his orders, as Geoff stripped. When he was naked, and Ben was in position, he made his way over to him. "Good boy."

He ran his hand down Ben's back, feeling the smooth and scarred skin against his palm. Geoff grabbed the lube from the drawer with his other hand and knelt behind him.

Geoff placed open mouth kisses along Ben's neck and shoulders, gently biting as he moved down Ben's back, listening to the moans Ben made every time he bit him. He looked up and grinned when he saw the marks he'd left on Ben's back. He hadn't broken the skin but anyone who saw them would know what they were. He stroked down Ben's ribs trailing his tongue across the base of his spine.

When he reached Ben's arse, he bit harder and heard Ben gasp above him, watching him grip the headboard in his hands. He grabbed Ben's cheeks and held them open as he blew on his hole. He lubed his fingers then rubbed one around the muscle waiting for it to relax a little before slowly pushing his finger in.

Geoff felt the slight resistance and gently moved it in and out until the muscle relaxed. He added another one and searched until he found Ben's spot, rubbing it, eliciting sounds of pleasure from Ben, feeling Ben's body tremble beneath his hands.

The most arousing part of this was knowing how much pleasure Ben received. He knew that Ben's time on the street hadn't been anywhere near enjoyable. Sex had been a job, nothing more, nothing less. Geoff wanted him to get as much enjoyment as he could out of their time together. He wanted to blow his mind with pleasure.

When he had three fingers in and Ben was relaxed, he pulled them out, rolled a condom on, quickly lubed it up then slowly pushed the head in. Once the head was in, he waited for Ben to adjust to him, stroking his back and hips. At eight inches, Geoff knew he wasn't small, and he didn't want to hurt Ben by shoving his dick in.

When he saw Ben nod, he pushed in slowly, inch by inch, until he was fully encased in Ben's warm, smooth arse and waited again. He leaned over, wrapping his arm around Ben, then pulled him up and back, so Ben sat on Geoff knees, his back against Geoff's chest.

Easing out slowly, Geoff thrust back in, holding on to Ben's hips and pulling him down at the same time. Ben started to move himself as he reached back, wrapping a hand around the back of Geoff's neck. He wanted to take his time and set a slow but steady rhythm, enjoying the feeling of being inside Ben. Listening to Ben's moans of pleasure, it wasn't long before Geoff found himself going faster and thrusting up into Ben harder.

"Sir, harder.....please...please..." Ben begged.

Geoff wrapped his other arm around Ben, grabbing Ben's cock, stroking it in time with his thrusts. The heat surrounding his cock inside Ben was indescribable. Hot and tight. Silky smooth. He slammed into Ben's sweet spot with every thrust, feeling Ben's cock harden even more in his hand. He groaned at the feelings Ben brought out in him and Geoff kissed Ben's back and neck, sucking on the flesh, marking it.

"Oh God!" Ben cried out.

He heard Ben's cries and knew he was getting close. He started to hammer into him and threw his head back as he hissed in pleasure. He'd never felt like this. The things he wanted to do with Ben; the things he wanted to do to Ben.

"Come for me," Geoff commanded as he continued to fuck him.

He heard Ben shout out then watched as ropes off come shot from Ben's cock onto his hand and up Ben's chest. Ben's hole clamped around him, squeezing his dick in a tight grip, causing Geoff to groan.

Geoff's balls pulled up tight, a tingling sensation spreading from them. Electricity shot up and around his shaft and groin, and Geoff came, pulses of come filling the condom. He moaned, pleasure flooding through him, jerking through his orgasm with no control of his body. Panting, Geoff dropped his head on Ben's shoulder, waiting for his heart to slow. Sweat covered his body and Geoff smiled, placing a kiss on Ben's shoulder. Damn, that was another amazing orgasm. The sex seemed to get hotter and better every time they were together.

When Geoff finally had control over his body, he eased Ben off of him, laid him down on the bed and then disposed of the condom. Grabbing the wipes, Geoff cleaned them both then lay down next to Ben, pulling him close. Kissing his head, he sighed in contentment listening to Ben's quiet breathing, indicating that he was asleep. It wasn't long before he joined him.

❋ ❋ ❋

Next day was busy for them both. Geoff made numerous phone calls to arrange Adam's funeral that involved speaking at length to the detective in charge of the case. There hadn't been any more attacks and the case was coming to a standstill. It was distasteful to think it, but it looked like another crime would have to be committed before they could move forward with the case. There was little or no DNA and most prostitutes attacked didn't want to report it to the police; they were having a hard time to find victims willing to talk.

Geoff sighed, leaning back in his chair in the study. Having listened to Ben talk about some of the things he'd witnessed when living on the streets, he could sympathise with the people still out there. They didn't trust anyone and found it hard to believe that the cops would be willing to help them, so they just didn't bother with them at all.

By mid-afternoon, he'd completed everything on his list and went to his bedroom to get ready for the function that night. He walked in to find Ben lying on the bed, hands behind his head, staring at the ceiling.

"You okay there?" Geoff asked, sitting next to Ben.

"Yeah. Trying to settle my nerves about tonight."

"I'll be with you the whole time."

"No, you won't." Ben smiled up at him. "Someone is going to drag you away, but it's okay, I understand."

Geoff grabbed Ben's hand and hauled him up from the bed. "Shower?" he asked, wriggling his eyebrows at Ben.

Ben laughed, which was the reaction Geoff had wanted. He dragged him into the bathroom and, after regulating the temperature in the shower, stripped off, watching Ben do the same.

He could see the difference in Ben's physique now. Weeks of eating decent food was paying off, and he'd started putting on some much-needed weight. He knew Ben had been working out with his free weights, and he had some nice definition now. He could see the six pack developing, and he now had great biceps. He watched Ben get in the shower then followed him in, closing the door behind in. He looked at Ben's wet body, and his blood went south. He stared down at his hard cock and heard Ben speak.

"Want some help with that, Sir?" He looked at Ben, smiling. Gripping his cock, he leaned back against the shower wall, stroking himself slowly. He watched Ben drop to his knees, taking his dick in his mouth. He threw his head back, banging it against the shower wall, but didn't pay any attention to it. Ben was doing wondrous things down there, and he knew it wouldn't be long before he came.

He watched Ben bob up and down, groaning when he saw Ben's cheeks hollow as he sucked him in. Ben twirled his tongue around the head of Geoff's dick then took him back in his mouth, swallowing around the head before he hummed. Fuck! He curled his toes as he felt the tingling start, and Geoff reached down to tug his balls to try and stop himself from coming, but it was too late.

"Oh, fuck, Ben, I'm coming..."

Shooting into Ben's mouth, Geoff gasped and watched Ben swallow every ribbon, moaning at the visual he presented on his knees. Geoff groaned at the sight as Ben stood licking his lips, removing all traces of Geoff's come. Geoff grabbed the sides of Ben's head, pulling him forward into a scorching hot kiss, moaning when he tasted himself on Ben's tongue.

"Let me clean you up," Ben muttered when he ended the kiss and stepped away.

He stood watching Ben clean him and wash his hair. It had been a long time since someone had made him feel this way and paid attention to his needs. It was just the little things Ben was doing, but it was also having Ben there when he came home that he looked forward to the most. His house no longer felt empty.

When Ben had finished, he returned the favour and then switched the shower off. He handed Ben a towel and got one for himself, wrapping it around his waist and walking into the bedroom.

He dressed quickly and was putting his tie on when his phone rang.

New Beginnings

"Hello."

"Hey, it's me." Harry told him. "Just wanted to remind you, that you're coming over for lunch tomorrow. Will Ben be coming as well?"

"Yes, we'll both be there. Elevenish alright for you?"

"That's fine. How're things between you two?"

"Great, but we're getting ready right now. Got that function tonight."

Harry snorted down the phone. "Rather you than me. God, I hated those things when we got dragged along with Dad."

"Yeah, I'm not fond of them myself, but it's a necessary evil."

"Well, have fun and we'll see you both tomorrow."

Geoff hung up and threw the phone on the bed. He turned to see Ben dressed. Fuck, did Ben look good in a suit. He could see how nervous Ben was by the way he fiddled with his cuff links.

"Here." He took the cuff links from him and put it through the holes in his sleeves. Noticing he hadn't put his tie on, he reached for it and turned Ben to face the mirror. Standing behind him, Geoff reached over his shoulders and put the tie on for him.

When he'd finished, Geoff ran his hands over Ben's shoulders and down his arms linking their fingers together. Ben leaned back into him, turning his head up towards him. Geoff kissed Ben's lips, opening his mouth and stroking Ben's tongue with his own. After a few minutes, he pulled back and looked into Ben's flushed face and lust-glazed eyes. He loved the fact that he could put that look on his face.

He turned Ben around in his arms and held him close, feeling his heartbeat against his chest. Looking at the clock, he pulled back, smiling at him. "Ready?"

"As I'll ever be." Ben gave a completely unconvincing smile that made Geoff laugh.

"You'd think you were going to your death. It won't be bad." The doorbell rang. "That's us."

"You're not driving?"

Shaking his head, Geoff answered, "Not tonight."

Geoff opened the front door to find the black limo parked out front. Holding Ben's hand, he pulled him towards it.

"Wow. We're going in that?" The awe was evident in Ben's voice as he stared at the limo. He ran a hand along it then glanced at the driver who was trying hard to contain a smile.

"Get in, Ben. There's more to see inside."

"If it's as nice as the outside, I think I'll come in my pants," Ben whispered to him.

Geoff burst out laughing as the driver held the door open for them. He followed Ben into the car and sat down opposite him on the black leather seats. He followed Ben as he touched everything, eyes wide open, staring in admiration.

"Do you want a drink?"

"They have drinks?" Ben gasped out.

"Yes. We have Champagne."

Ben nodded quickly. "Please."

Geoff poured them both a glass and raised his glass towards Ben. "To us." He stared into Ben's eyes.

"To us."

New Beginnings

Chapter Sixteen

They pulled up outside the Lowry Hotel and waited as the driver opened the door for them. Ben stared at the building in front of him and hadn't realised how long he'd stood there for until he felt Geoff take his hand, squeezing it tightly. The building was glass-fronted and didn't have the typical straight look. It curved in the centre and, to Ben, it looked beautiful and modern.

They walked into the wide and spacious foyer, and they heard Geoff's name immediately called. Holding onto his hand, Ben followed behind Geoff as he moved through the crowd and continued to glance around the room. There were pillars in the centre of the room, with the reception against the wall and a seating area off to the side.

"Hi, Geoff. Can you remember which room we're in?"

Ben turned back to face Geoff when he heard the question.

"I think it's the Compass Room." Geoff turned to him. "Ben, this is

Ethan Woods. He owns Woods Solicitors. We went to University together. Ethan this is my partner, Ben."

Ben squirmed under the intense stare Ethan gave him and found himself leaning into Geoff for support. Tall with dark blond hair and brown eyes so dark they almost appeared black, Ethan continued to look at him as Ben stared back.

Finally, Ethan held his hand out. "Hi, Ben, I hope you know what you're getting into being with Geoff here."

Ben wiped his hand on his pants before he shook Ethan's and attempted to smile at him. "Erm, yeah."

Ethan laughed and slapped Geoff on the back. "I like him. Where did you find him?" Seeing the look on Geoff's face, he added, "Oh, when you said Ben, I didn't think it was the same Ben."

"What?" Ben glared at Geoff, pulling his hand free. Had he told someone about him?

Geoff turned to face him, running his hands up and down Ben's arms. "Ethan knows. He's one of my closest friends, and I trust him. He'll never repeat anything that I've said to him."

"Hey, don't get upset with Geoff. I coerced the information out of him. It doesn't matter to me what you did. You're here now and from what Geoff has said, getting your life back on track. He said you're going to go to college. What are you planning on studying?"

Ben didn't know how to answer him. Geoff hadn't said anything about talking to someone about him, and he was furious that he had. He felt Geoff take his hand and squeeze it.

"The sciences and maths," he answered tersely.

"Awesome. My sister's at Uni studying engineering. She's the smart one in the family. Just don't tell her I said that or I'll never hear the end of it."

"I'll just get us some drinks. Stay here with Ethan and I'll be back in a minute," Geoff told him, walking away.

Ben stared after Geoff, his mouth falling open he watched Geoff walk away. How could he leave him here with someone he didn't know? He smiled nervously at Ethan, fiddling with his cuff links, trying desperately to think what to say.

"So, you're starting college in September?"

Ben nodded, scanning the room for Geoff. Why couldn't he find him? "Yeah."

"Nervous, excited."

"A bit of both really."

"Oh, see that woman over there? Black dress, blonde hair scraped up?"

Ben looked at where Ethan was pointing then nodded. "Yeah, why?"

"Avoid her like the plague. She's a complete bitch. In fact, there's a lot of people to avoid at these functions, but it's something that has to be done."

"Why?" These functions were new to Ben, and any advice would be great.

"Business. Not everyone here is a solicitor. Lots of different industries are here tonight. You come, make contacts, and hopefully gain some new clients. You have to smile and play nice but there are plenty of sharks here too, so stick with Geoff or me and we'll take care of you."

"Why would you take care of me?" Ben asked him, frowning.

"Geoff is my closest friend and he has feelings for you. I'll admit at first when he told me all about you, I thought he was a fucking idiot to take you in and try to help you out. Then you left, and I saw the state he was in, but you came back, and I have to ask why?" Ethan tilted his head, staring at Ben. "Why did you come back? I know you took money from him, not that it bothered Geoff. Did you run out? Did something happen on the streets and you realised that living at Geoff's was better? What was it?" He continued to stare at Ben, waiting for an answer.

Ben shrugged, looking away. He didn't know this man, so why should he tell him anything? Ben sighed. Ethan clearly had Geoff's best interest at heart and was looking out for his friend. That was why he was asking the questions. He didn't want to see his friend being used or hurt. He knew about Ben's past, so where was the harm? Would it be so bad to tell him?

"I think I needed to go back, I can't explain it. I was, I guess, depressed over Adam and I felt guilty that things seemed to be getting better for me, and he was dead. Sounds stupid, I know." Ben shrugged.

"No, I don't think it sounds stupid. Something similar happened to a friend of ours when we were at Uni."

"Really? Geoff's never mentioned it." Ben looked up at Ethan.

"No, I doubt he will. Let's just say he understands more than he lets on."

Just as Ben was about to ask another question, a noise off to the side caught their attention and then everyone started walking towards the conference rooms. Ben looked around for Geoff and saw him walking behind with two glasses in his hands. He came up beside him and handed him one.

"What's happening now?" Ben asked him.

"We're just moving to the rooms where the conference will take place, then everyone will continue to mingle. At some point, we'll sit down while someone else will talk a lot of shit that will bore us to tears. But you have to look interested, and then there will be a buffet, and people will mingle again."

"Ethan said it's to meet people and drum up clients."

"It's called networking." Geoff sighed. "A necessary evil."

Ben sipped his drink, watching Geoff meet a hell of a lot of people. He smiled at everyone and shook hands, pretending to be interested in what they were saying when really he couldn't wait to leave. Sure enough, thirty minutes later, the speeches started and he sat next to Geoff. At one point he was nudged awake; he hadn't realised he had fallen asleep. He looked up at Geoff sheepishly and shrugged. All of this meant jack shit to him and he was so bored!

Once the speeches had ended, and boy, were they long and droning, they started mingling again. Geoff went to the buffet table to get them some food and he scanned the room, seeing Ethan in the corner talking to a group of people. When their eyes met, Ethan gave him the thumbs up sign. He returned it and took the plate from Geoff when he returned from the buffet table.

"I thought you'd have a sit-down meal?"

"Depends on who's organised it. I prefer this as it allows you to eat quickly, do what you have to do, then leave. I'm not a fan of these."

When they had finished the food, Ben followed Geoff around as he did his meet and greet. He smiled politely at the few people he'd already been introduced to and attempted to make conversation. He felt so completely out of his depth, but Geoff stayed with him and was constantly touching him to reassure him. It was at this time that he scanned the room and Ben saw him.

Ben's whole body came to complete stop. What the fuck was he doing here? He started to sweat and his heart hammered in his chest. He swallowed at the bile that was suddenly in his throat. Fuck, someone from his street time. A punter, someone who'd come to him regularly. A sick, twisted fuck who got off on inflicting some form of pain. He wouldn't have gone with him after that first time, but the money he'd paid... He turned away, praying that he hadn't noticed him.

There was no God. Ben heard his voice as he said hello to Geoff and asked to be introduced. Ben turned and plastered the biggest, fakest smile he could on his face and held his hand out. The punter, Edward Chambers, held his hand and ran his thumb over the back of it, smiling slyly at Ben. He snatched his hand back and grabbed Geoff's, squeezing it tightly. He saw Geoff frown at him.

"Excuse us, Edward, but Ethan is waving for us. It was a pleasure to see you again."

As he walked through the throng of people Geoff whispered to him. "Are you alright?"

"Just feel a bit off. Do you know where the toilets are?"

Geoff looked around the room before pointing to a sign over one of the doors. "Over there. Are you sure you're alright? You look pale."

Ben tried to smile as he answered him, "I'm fine. I just need a minute."

Geoff nodded, still frowning slightly. "I'll see you back here then. I'll be with Ethan."

Ben gave a weak smile and walked towards the bathroom, keeping his head down to avoid making eye contact with anyone. Once he made it inside, he locked himself in a cubicle and, putting the lid down, sat and dropped his head in his hands. He groaned. How could he be so stupid? He knew what some of the people were like who paid for rent boys. Some made a lot of money and held high-powered jobs. Why did he think he wouldn't see anyone like that here? Why hadn't he even thought about it?

He heard the door to the toilets open and held his breath. He listened as the doors to the other cubicles were opened then heard him speak.

"Come out, Ben. I know you're in there."

Edward. Why had he followed him in here?

Ben unlocked the door and cracked it open, peering round the edge of the door itself. Edward stood there, hands in his pants pockets, staring at him. He took a hand out of his pants and waved Ben over.

"Come on. There's no need to hide in there."

Ben walked out of the cubicle and stood in front of him. What did he want?

"So, I see you've moved up in the world. Imagine my surprise when I saw you with Geoff. It made me wonder if he knew about you, about what you are." He stepped forward and stroked the lapel of Ben's suit, causing him to stumble back away from him. Edward smirked at him. "You might be wearing better clothing, but you are still nothing more than a whore. How many times did I fuck you? How much did you cost me? I wondered where you had gone. You were the only one who I really enjoyed." He stepped back into Ben's personal space, pushing him back against the wall, holding him there with his hands on his shoulders. "I've missed you. The way I could you make you whimper. The way I could make you cry. No one else responds like you do. No one else feels the way you do."

Edward leaned forward and licked Ben's cheek. Ben turned his head away, trying to push him back, but Edward grabbed his hands and held them, forcing them above his head and squeezing them tight. He pushed his body into Ben's and licked his ear as he whispered to him.

"I've tried for almost two years now to get Geoff to sell to me, and he always refused, but seeing you, well, I think he might see things differently now, don't you? I can't imagine you'll want people to know what you are, and can you imagine how that would affect Geoff and his family's business? A business his father started and Geoff is continuing. Do you think his clients would want to stay with him when they know he's fucking a whore? Once he knows that you're nothing but a broken down, used hole, he'll get rid of you." Edward paused then continued, "Now, you know your place. Down on your knees." He let go of Ben's hands and went to open his pants.

The door to the toilets opened, and Edward pushed away from Ben, smiling as he turned around. Ben watched him walk out of the toilet and shuddered, releasing the breath he'd been holding. What the fuck was he going to do?

Walking over to the sink, Ben turned the tap on, noticing how badly his hands were shaking. He held them under the running water hoping the heat would warm them. He gave a shaky smile to the man who'd come in as he washed his hands and left the toilets.

His stomach suddenly heaved, and he barely managed to make it to the toilet before being violently sick. When he finished, he spat out, resisting the urge to vomit again when he could taste the residue of sick in his mouth. He wiped his mouth with some toilet roll before staggering to his feet and flushing the toilet. He went back to the sink and washed his mouth out with cold water, trying to get rid of the taste of vomit. He leaned over the sink, trying to hold himself up on wobbly legs, staring at his reflection in the mirror.

His face looked washed out, pale and sweaty. As he stared at himself in the mirror, the door opened, and Geoff walked in, looking concerned when he saw him.

"Are you alright? You've been gone a few minutes."

"Yeah, sorry. Got a bit nervous. There are a lot of people. I guess I'm not used to the crowds."

"I'm sorry. I should have thought about how this would be for you.

I guess I wanted to show you off a little." Geoff moved forward, pulling Ben into a hug.

Ben smiled up at him, "Really?"

"Really. You, Ben Parker, are a handsome young man. I think you're fucking hot. Can't wait to get you home tonight and show you just how hot I think you are."

Ben felt butterflies in his stomach at the thought of being with Geoff again. He loved having sex with him, which was strange given his past. He even loved the thought of being dominated by him. Someone else taking control so he could let go. He'd had to be in control for so long that it felt liberating to hand it over to Geoff. When he had grown to trust him, he wasn't sure, but he certainly did now. This brought up his current predicament: Edward.

"How long do we have to stay?" he asked Geoff. He wanted to get away as soon as he could. The further away from Edward, the better. He didn't want to have to speak to him again.

"Another hour tops. Can you manage that long?"

Ben leaned into Geoff, taking a deep breath, smelling his cologne. He nodded into his chest. "Yeah," he mumbled.

Geoff stepped back from him, holding his hand out. "Come on then. The sooner we go out there, the sooner we can leave."

Ben slid his hand into Geoff's and let Geoff pull him out of the toilet. The next hour was torturous for Ben. He found himself constantly searching the room to see if he could locate Edward in the crowd. Once or twice they made eye contact and Edward would smile smugly at him and raise his glass in a sarcastic toast. Ben would look away quickly, breaking eye contact as soon as he could.

The entire time they circulated, Ben tried to control of his stomach. He had to keep wiping his sweaty palms on his suit pants furtively and smile nicely at everyone Geoff introduced him to. He had the smile plastered on his face for so long his jaw was beginning to ache. He wanted this to be over and done with so they could leave.

Finally, after what felt like an eternity later, Geoff told him they would be leaving. Ethan weaved his way through the crowds and walked with them as they attempted to leave. But, every few steps someone would stop either of them to enquire how they were, completely fake if you asked Ben, but he guessed this was what you had to do. When the Holy Grail was in sight, the door, Edward appeared, like a magician in front of them, smiling in a smug, slimy way.

"Leaving so soon, Geoff?"

"Yes. It's been a beneficial night all round. How has it been for you?"

Edward glanced at Ben, smirking. "Oh, it's definitely had its highlights. I was wondering when we could meet up, discuss some business propositions."

"If it's to discuss my selling the business or some form of merger, then I think we'd be wasting our time. The answer is still no."

"I think you should think about it, don't you think so, Ben? I'll have my secretary call you Monday to arrange it."

Ben stared straight ahead as Edward merged with the crowds. He felt Geoff grab his arm and start to pull him out.

"What was that about?" Ethan asked Geoff as they exited the hotel.

"In the car," Geoff ordered.

Once they had reached the limo, the driver opened the door, and all three got in.

"How does he know you, Ben?"

Chapter Seventeen

Ben looked at Geoff, who faced him across the limo.

"What? You know Edward, Ben?" Ethan asked him.

Ben swallowed. "Yeah."

"Fuck. Was he was a customer?" Ethan asked as he sat back on the seat, shaking his head.

Ben nodded, looking down at his clasped hands. The knuckles had turned white; he was holding them so tightly. He saw Geoff's hands close over his and gently pry them open.

"Tell us everything," Geoff demanded softly.

Ben looked up, glancing between the two of them. He shook his head, sitting back in the seat, pulling his hands free from Geoff's. "I can't," he whispered.

Ethan snorted. "We need to know, Ben. I can't imagine this is easy for you, but Edward is up to something. I could see the way he looked at you when he was talking to Geoff. Like he knew something we didn't, something he could use."

"He paid me, okay? He knew me as soon as he saw me. Cornered me in the toilets, threatened to tell everyone about us if I didn't do what he wanted." Ben blurted it out in a rush. "I'm sorry."

"You've nothing to apologise for," Geoff told him as he sat back. "What are you thinking, Ethan?"

"This is exactly what he's needed. He'll use this one way or the other. I wouldn't be surprised if he mentions this in the meeting with you and threatens you with it. We both know he wants a merger with you or for you to sell." Ethan turned to face Ben. "Ben, what did he say? Can you remember?"

Ben looked at the floor nodding. "Yeah, he wants Geoff's business and..." He couldn't finish.

"He wants you." Ethan finished for him.

Ben looked up, startled that Ethan knew. "I don't know why. There are plenty of us on the street for him to have."

"I saw the way he looked at you. You don't have to be a genius to figure out what he wants and he wants you. Two for one. He gets the merger, and he gets Ben."

"Not going to happen," Geoff stated vehemently. "Ben is mine and I don't share."

"No! You can't say that! He threatened you. He said he could ruin you by telling everyone what I am!" Ben practically shouted at him.

"What you were, and I'm not ashamed of you or your actions. What's in the past is exactly that. It's the past, and you survived a pretty fucked up one. We will figure this out."

New Beginnings

"Damn straight we will. Drop me off at mine and I'll come round tomorrow. We can brainstorm the shit out of this then," Ethan told them sternly. "I won't have that cunt fuck with my friends."

Ben watched Ethan as he stared out of the window, face hard and arms crossed over his chest. Geoff smirked at him then winked.

"We'll sort this out. I'd tell you not to worry, but that won't stop you, will it?"

Geoff moved over and sat next to Ben, pulling him into his arms and holding him tight as he kissed his head. "I don't regret a thing between us," he murmured into his hair.

They dropped Ethan off at his house with his promise that he would be round in the morning, and then they carried on home. Ben sat quietly in the car, contemplating what he was going to do. He couldn't let Edward ruin Geoff, not after everything he'd done for him. That left him with no other choice but to leave.

"I know what you're thinking, and the answer is no, you're not leaving," Geoff told him.

"It's for the best! Edward will try to use me to ruin you! Your family has worked too hard for it to be taken from you because of me," Ben pleaded with him.

"No. What Edward is doing is blackmail, and I'm pretty sure we'll come up with a plan tomorrow. We don't even know for certain what he's going to do. How will he tell people about you without revealing how he knows you? I'm certain he won't out himself, so let's see what we can come up with first."

They pulled up outside Geoff's and Ben walked to the house while Geoff spoke to the driver. He watched as the limo drove off, and Geoff came up beside him and opened the door. They walked into the house, and Ben closed his eyes. His body was heavy like lead weights had been attached to his limbs, and it was difficult to move.

Geoff walked into the kitchen, and Ben slowly followed him. He watched Geoff open the fridge and took out a couple of bottles of water. Passing one to Ben, he nodded to the chair and Ben sat down.

Geoff sat opposite him. "Tell me about the two of you. I need to know everything."

"You want to do this now?" Ben's shoulders slumped. Why go through this now? Couldn't they do it tomorrow? He just wanted to go to bed.

"Do you want to do this tomorrow? In front of everyone?"

Well, when put like that....no. "Okay, I understand, but I don't know how this will help you."

Leaning on the table, Geoff told Ben, "I won't be going in blind. He could say anything to me, and I wouldn't know if it was the truth. I trust you, Ben. I need you to trust me in this."

Ben looked away, thinking about what he had said. Could he trust Geoff? He couldn't deny that there was a certain level of trust between him. The things he let Geoff do to him...

"You know you can trust me, Ben. You wouldn't have come back here when you left if you didn't trust me."

Ben looked back at Geoff, realising he was right. He did trust him, but he was scared. Scared of how Geoff would look at him after he told him what Edward liked, what he had let him do to him. He dominated, like Geoff, but with Geoff, it was consensual and at no point had he felt like he couldn't stop things if he wanted to. With Edward, he'd been in complete control, and Edward got off on that control and on inflicting pain. On making Ben feel powerless and terrified.

Coughing slightly, he nodded, "Okay. I just... I don't want you to hate me."

"Why would I hate you?" Geoff asked him, frowning. "I know a lot of what you've done and I'm still here."

"I know, but the things I let him do... it humiliates me to think I let him do those things, but I needed the money, and he paid a lot and I mean a lot. One job with him and I didn't have to sell myself for at least a week. I don't know why he kept coming back to me when he could have bought anyone."

"Maybe he saw something in you."

"I don't understand," Ben admitted.

"A vulnerability. People like him can pick up on it." Geoff paused, taking a deep breath and then blew it out heavily. "So, tell me. Tell me everything."

Ben also took a deep breath, shuddering inwardly at the thought of talking about it. He cleared his throat. "He would pick me up and take me back to some cheap hotel. Didn't want to do it in the car or some alley. He preferred privacy and time." He paused, thinking about how he could tell Geoff what he had allowed Edward to do to him.

"As soon as we were in the room, he would have me strip and then shower. Once I was done, he would tie me to the bed, face down." Ben swallowed, his stomach churning. "He liked to inflict pain, so he would use things on me, whip me, and bite me. Never enough to leave permanent marks, but enough that I would cry out. The more noise I made, the more he enjoyed it. Then he would fuck me. No lube. He wanted me to feel it. Liked to make me bleed. Liked to make me cry. He got off on that. The tears and the blood." Ben had to swallow again. Breathing deeply for a few seconds, he continued. "When he finished, he would shower, release the ropes holding me down then throw the money in my face with a smirk on his. Sometimes he would use toys and he would... fuck me... with them... as hard as he could." Ben shuddered and closed his eyes. "It could have been worse. I've heard stories of some guys left scarred, I mean, really fucked up and ending up in the hospital." Ben opened his eyes but didn't look at Geoff. He didn't want to see the revulsion on his face.

"So Edward likes to humiliate and inflict pain. He likes being in control and gets off on it," Geoff murmured quietly as he reached across and squeezed Ben's hand. "You let me use cuffs."

"Trust," Ben whispered back to him, watching him as he peeled the label of his bottle.

"Yes, that sounds like him. He always likes to be in control and always gives the impression he's more important than he is. He never left you with any scars?"

"No, not that it mattered. I have plenty of scars but each time we were together, it would be worse than the last. So, I guess it was just a matter of time before he did."

"I agree."

Ben's eyebrows shot up. "You do?"

"It sounds like he's just starting."

"I don't understand." Ben looked at Geoff as his eyebrows hunched together. Just starting?

"Middle-aged man. Supposedly happily married. You said every session was worse than the last. So he's just getting started, learning what he likes. You need to remember, I've been doing this for a while now. I've been to those types of clubs..."

"Those clubs?" Ben interrupted him.

"BDSM clubs."

"Oh! The clubs you told me about." Ben nodded. He remembered Geoff talking to him about it.

"As I said when I explained them to you, I haven't been for a while now."

"Because of me."

"Partly." Geoff agreed. "Anyway, I've seen his type at the club. They don't listen to safe words, always pushing past the subs hard lines or limits. These places are heavily monitored. I don't need to tell you why, do I?"

Ben shook his head. "No, I guess you wouldn't want people to be hurt."

"Unless they wanted it, and it was specified in their contract."

"Like the one you gave me."

"Yes. People like Edward would ignore what the sub wanted or didn't want. Edward seems to like inflicting pain. Soon he will want to leave marks, cause damage. Mark his property."

"I think I'm gonna be sick." Ben took a deep breath as the queasiness in his stomach intensified. If he was still on the streets, seeing Edward...

"You've had a lucky escape, but I wonder who he's with now." Geoff scratched his chin. "Edward tied you up, but you don't have a problem with me."

"No. I know you won't hurt me, not like Edward. And he wants me back." Ben swallowed hard. No way was Edward ever touching him again.

"He probably considers you as his."

"Fuck. Geoff, I should leave." Ben groaned, dropping his head into his hands.

"I've told you that you're staying."

"I can't," he whispered. Surely Geoff could see that? Ben wasn't worth Geoff losing his business over, having his name and image tarnished. "I'm used goods, worthless, broken. Please see that?"

"You're not. Why can't you see what I see, Ben? Why can't you see who you are? You're not broken, and whatever comes our way, we will face it together as a team because that's what we are." Geoff told him sincerely.

"What about your business?"

"A team," Geoff repeated.

"Really," Ben whispered.

Geoff smiled slightly at him. "Yes, really. You and me. Come on. Let's go to bed and we can face this tomorrow."

Geoff stood holding out his hand to Ben, waiting. Ben put his hand in Geoff's and let Geoff pull him up and out of the room. When they entered the bedroom, Geoff turned on the small lamp and undressed Ben. Ben stood there watching him, noticing the care Geoff took with him. Once he was naked, Geoff laid him on the bed and also undressed, then lay down beside him, pulling the covers over them. Pulling Ben close and folding him in his arms, Geoff kissed Ben on his head. Such care. No wonder Ben loved him.

"Go to sleep, Ben. Things will be better in the morning."

Chapter Eighteen

Ben woke the next morning to the sound of voices coming from downstairs. Rolling over, he looked at the clock, realising it was almost eleven. Standing up, he grabbed some sweatpants and a top and put them on. He took a leak in the bathroom and brushed his teeth before going downstairs.

Walking into the kitchen, he was surprised by who was there. He was expecting Ethan and Geoff, but not Tom and Seb. They all turned and smiled at him as he walked in. He stopped, frowning at them. He felt like prey, the way they were all smiling at him.

"Why all the smiles?" he asked, frowning slightly.

"No reason," Geoff told him, walking over and kissing him.

"So, I guess everyone now knows huh? Great," Ben muttered as he looked away.

"It's not like that," Geoff assured him.

Ben pulled back, staring up at Geoff. "Really? I understand why Ethan is here, but not Tom and Seb." Glancing over at them, Ben added, "No offence, guys."

"None taken," Seb assured him.

"Geoff called us because I have the same experience as you, so he figured I could help," Tom told him.

"We just want to help, Ben. When I told Tom, he wanted to come straight over," Seb said.

"Yeah, we don't need his shit. And there isn't much I didn't experience on the streets." Tom looked down at his trainers, rubbing the toes of one on the floor. Seb reached over and gripped Tom's hand.

"No, I get it. More heads, right? I just wasn't expecting everyone and it kinda threw me." Ben shrugged, rubbing the back of his head with his hand.

"Let's sit in the living room," Geoff told them, reaching for Ben's hand and pulling him towards the living room.

Once they were all sat down, Ethan turned to face them. "I've been thinking about this. This is the way I see it. Edward will use Ben any way he can to get what he wants. He wants your business, and he wants Ben. I'm certain he'll attempt some form of blackmail."

"We should call the police," Seb told them. "They'll be able to help."

"We can't say for certain what Edward will do. It's only an assumption on our part at the moment. We need to wait and see if he contacts me and arranges a meeting. If he uses it to blackmail me, then we can go to the police," Geoff told Seb.

"I don't want to speak to the cops. I don't want to tell them what he put me through," Ben whispered.

"We might not have a choice, Ben. If he attempts to blackmail me, the police will need to know everything and that includes what happened between both of you." Geoff spoke to him gently.

Ben stood up, pacing the floor, running his hands through his hair. He didn't want to go to the police and tell them about Edward. He knew how they would look at him. Like he was scum. He'd seen it before when they'd questioned him over Adam. He didn't want to go through that again. But he couldn't let Edward use him to hurt Geoff either. The situation didn't leave him with much choice.

Ben should leave. He should get as far away as possible, and then none of this would affect Geoff or his business.

He looked at Geoff, smiling wanly. He couldn't let on what he was thinking, otherwise Geoff would try to stop him. He should have let Geoff fall asleep last night and then left. There would be none of this now. He could have just left a note and been gone before Geoff woke up. Where, he didn't know, but it had to be better than putting Geoff in the position he was in now.

"So, you're going to have a meeting with him and see what he does? Then go to the police," Ben asked Geoff.

"Yes. If he doesn't say anything, we can say we were wrong. However, if he does use you, I can tell him I'll think about it and then go to the police. You can tell them how you know Edward and what he said to you when we were at the function."

"I can go with you as well. I saw you get into his car remember? We laughed about it. Talked about how he was compensating." Tom smiled at him. "Look, I don't want to go to the fuckin' cops and rake it all up. I feel like I'm finally moving forward and getting on with my life, but I can't let someone like that fuckwit do this to you and Geoff. I'll help and I'll go to the cops with you too."

"Wow, babe." Seb smiled at Tom pulling him in to hold him tight.

"I'll come as well, if you need me too."

Ben watched Tom return the gesture and smile softly at Seb as he nodded.

"You would do that, Tom?" Ben asked quietly. He didn't want Tom to be dragged into this too.

"Yeah, I would. We have a chance at something better, and I don't want to see it ruined by some fuckin' cunt who thinks he can use our past to get something he doesn't have a right to. This situation doesn't just affect Geoff. It affects Seb and me too."

Ben dropped down onto the chair staring at Tom. He was right. He hadn't thought about it like that. If anything happened and Geoff ended up selling his business or having to do this merger thing, then Seb or Tom could lose their jobs.

"Don't think leaving will change any of this," Ethan suddenly said.

"What?" Ben looked at Ethan, startled at his insight. How did he know?

"You think if you're not here then Edward won't try to do blackmail, Ben? He's seen you with Geoff, hell, most people there saw you two together. All Edward has to do is start a few rumours, make certain comments and it'll spread. It will have a knock-on effect."

Ben sighed, slumping in the chair. So, leaving wouldn't help. Still, he didn't want to go to the cops, but if Tom was willing to do it, then he could man up as well. Running his fingers over his lips, Ben dropped his head back on the chair, sighing deeply.

"So, what's the plan then?" he asked, lifting his head to look at each of them.

"Well, we see if Edward arranges a meeting first. If he does, then we wait and see if he mentions his relationship with you." Geoff stopped talking when Ben snorted at the word 'relationship.' "I want to know what exactly he is going to do with the knowledge of what you did. Is he going for a merger or will he try to buy me out?" Geoff shrugged. "Once we know which way he's going to play this, then we can go to the police and start the ball rolling."

"My guess would be that they have you arrange another meeting then they'll listen in," Ethan told them.

"Should we speak to the detective in charge of Adam's murder? She knows us, right?" Seb asked Geoff.

"Good point. Yeah, we should go to her. I think I have her card somewhere."

"So, Geoff." Ethan looked at Geoff and waggled his eyebrows.

Geoff sighed and stood up. "Alright, I'll get cooking."

They all ended up in the kitchen eating, and not long after, Ethan, Seb and Tom left, leaving Ben alone with Geoff. He watched him as he cleaned the kitchen thinking about how the week would play out. Would Edward arrange a meeting? Yeah, of course he would. He had seemed like the kind of person who would use whatever information he had to his advantage, and it was clear he had been after Geoff's business for a while now. Ben hated the fact that he was now causing problems for Geoff. The man had done so much for him, and now it seemed that a relationship was developing between them. He was excited and scared by that prospect. For the first time, he was having sex he actually enjoyed. Geoff made sure he enjoyed it. Yes, he was dominant, and they hadn't even truly begun to explore all that that entailed, but he knew he wanted to; he wanted Geoff to own him. Boy, that was a scary thought. After everything he had been through, he wanted to belong to Geoff and vice versa.

A shadow fell over him, and he looked up, seeing Geoff stood there with his hand held out to him, a slight smile on his face. He put his hand in Geoff's and allowed him to pull him up and out of the room. He led Ben to their bedroom and into the bathroom where he let go. Ben watched as he turned the shower on and checked the temperature. Once he was happy with it, he proceeded to undress, and when naked, he helped Ben out of his clothes.

Ben stood in the shower and let the water flow over him, closing his eyes. When he felt movement behind him, Ben opened his eyes, watching Geoff reach for the shampoo. He closed his eyes as Geoff washed his hair and then rinsed it.

Geoff took a washcloth and began to clean him, turning him around to clean his back. Ben felt so relaxed and peaceful. When Geoff had finished cleaning him, he switched the shower off and reached for a towel, drying them both.

Geoff led him to the bed and Ben lay down on it. He watched as Geoff opened the drawer and pulled out the handcuffs. He shivered, his dick hardening, knowing what was about to come.

"Stay there. I'll be back."

※ ※ ※

Geoff went to the kitchen, put some oil in the microwave and while it heated, took some ice cubes out of the freezer and put them in a glass. When the oil was warm enough, he took that and the glass of ice and walked back to the bedroom. He placed them on the bedside cabinet in full view of Ben.

Geoff held up the cuffs and looked at Ben, waiting for him to tell him he could continue. When Ben nodded, he cuffed one of his hands and then looped it through the headboard before attaching the cuff to his other wrist. Ben tested the cuffs, and nodded to Geoff. They weren't too tight. Geoff went back to the drawer and pulled out a blindfold.

"Safe word?"

"Dark."

"Dark?" Geoff asked in a puzzled tone.

"I'm afraid of the dark. So, if you do something I'm not sure of, I'll know to say it."

"Are you sure about wearing a blindfold?"

Ben nodded. "Yes, positive. I know it's you and I trust you."

"Dark, it is. What's your safe word for me to slow down?"

"Grey."

Geoff tied the blindfold and sat back, watching Ben's breathing settle back to normal. He looked so beautiful. Stretched out naked on his bed. Hands cuffed and blindfolded. He turned towards the drawer and took out a feather, the tube of lube and a small dildo. He wanted to show Ben pleasure and eradicate Edward from his thoughts. Going to the bathroom, he grabbed a towel and put it by the side of the bed. He lubed up the dildo and put it on a towel. He sat down next to Ben and slowly stroked up his left leg, running his knuckles over his balls, bypassing his dick and stroking up his chest. He tweaked both nipples until the nubs were hard and then reached for the feather.

He slowly stroked over Ben's nipple with the end of the feather and Ben jerked slightly. He continued to slowly stroke it over his nipples, then sucked one into his mouth. Releasing it, Geoff blew across it, watching it pebble. Ben gasped above him, and Geoff smiled to himself. He wanted him to enjoy the different sensations.

He continued to use the feather for another couple of minutes then switched to the ice. He rolled one over Ben's nipple and watched as Ben jerked and groaned.

"Sir..."

"Shush. Trust me."

He put a cube in his mouth let it melt for a minute before he started to place open mouth kisses over Ben's torso. He wanted Ben to feel the cold and wet from the cube. He watched goose bumps pop up over Ben's skin. When the cube had melted, he put another one in his mouth and sucked the head of Ben's cock into his mouth. Ben jerked again, and Geoff heard the cuffs rattle against the bars of the headboard.

"Fuck, Geoff...Sir..." Ben moaned above him.

Geoff used his tongue to move the cube all around Ben's cock until it had dissolved then rubbed lube around Ben's hole before gently pushing a finger in. Ben whimpered above him, clearly enjoying what he was doing to his body.

Reaching for the dildo, Geoff removed his finger and pushed the dildo in, switching it on. Ben jerked, moaning loudly. Geoff left him for a few seconds then returned, pouring warm oil over Ben's balls and around the base of his cock. Ben was making plenty of noise now pulling on the cuffs causing them to rattle.

Popping another cube into his mouth and pouring more oil into his hand, Geoff started to jack Ben off while sucking Ben's cock into his mouth. Ben screamed out above, sounding incoherent. The different temperatures on his cock and the vibrating dildo in his arse were pushing him towards his orgasm.

Geoff lifted his head and let the head drop out. "You can't come yet."

"What? No, no, no. I need to come! Please, fuck, I need it!" Ben begged him as he shook his head.

"I'm waiting."

Geoff watched Ben try to gain some control, his breathing rapid and his legs moving on the sheets. After a couple of minutes, Ben seemed to gain some control as his movement and breathing slowed.

"Do you want to continue?"

"Yes, Sir."

Geoff turned the dildo to a higher setting, put more ice cubes in his mouth, and continued with the blow job. He bobbed up and down then took Ben all the way in. He could hear and feel how this was affecting Ben, and fuck, he was so turned on, he didn't think he would have to touch himself. He was ready to explode.

Ben was so responsive. He was shaking above him, moaning loudly and thrashing his head. Geoff looked up at him. "Come." Ben's hips shot up off the bed, and Geoff swallowed as Ben came, crying out loudly, pulling on the cuffs as his arms strained. When Ben finally slumped down on the bed, Geoff switched the dildo off and carefully removed it, placing it on the towel. He took some wipes and cleaned Ben up, then removed the blindfold. As Geoff removed the cuffs, Ben blinked slowly above him, but kept his eyes closed. Geoff rubbed Ben's wrist, lowering his arms to Ben's sides.

Ben lay on the bed with his mouth slightly open, and eyes closed while he panted. Geoff wrapped him in his arms and held him, rubbing his back as he slowly calmed down. Kissing his head, he asked him, "Do you want some water?"

When Ben mumbled yes, Geoff reached over and picked the bottle up off the floor. He opened it and passed it to Ben. He held him up as Ben took several sips before he lay back down.

"Wow. I never..." Ben stopped talking.

"How are you doing?"

Ben nodded. "Yeah, I feel amazing, but tired. I never knew..." Ben stopped talking again and shook his head.

"I'm glad you enjoyed it," Geoff told him, stroking the hair from Ben's face.

Ben waved a hand in the general direction of his dick. "What about you? Do you need me to...?"

"No." Geoff interrupted him. "This was for you. Sleep. I'll wake you later."

Ben nodded, sighing deeply and, within minutes, was asleep. Geoff watched as he slept, running his fingers through his hair and stroking his chest. Ben had come to mean so much to him, and he didn't want to lose him now, not when he felt like his life was finally complete. Ben completed him. Geoff snorted, completed him. Fuck, Ben owned him. If someone had told him a year ago that a teenager would own him, mind and body, he would have laughed. But now, he didn't want to live his life without Ben in it.

He knew they had a tough couple of weeks ahead, and he wasn't sure what the outcome would be, but he knew one thing. Ben would be with him. He just needed to make sure Ben knew and believed that as well.

Chapter Nineteen

It was Thursday before Geoff told Ben he'd received a call from Edward's secretary that day, and they had arranged a meeting for the following Monday. Edward had apparently wanted a meeting for the following day, but Geoff had stated that at such short notice he was unable to accommodate him.

Ben didn't know why he had left it for so long. He would have expected him to call first thing Monday morning considering he knew what Ben had done and would use it to harm Geoff, but Geoff had told him it was a waiting game. Edward had purposefully waited to see how Geoff would react. They were sat eating dinner as Geoff explained what had happened to him.

"And nothing was said?" Ben asked him.

"No. His secretary didn't mention what the meeting was about. He's obviously taken his time in contacting me to make me wonder what he knows."

"You're not worried about it?" Ben was worried as he didn't want to cause any more problems than he already had. Biting his lip, Ben waited for Geoff to respond.

"No. We've got this covered. You know that, Ben. Stop worrying."

"I don't want you to be affected by my past and it's my past that's causing this now."

"No, it's Edward causing this, not you or your past. We're not doing anything wrong here, Ben, he is. If he attempts to use you to force me do something I don't want to, that's blackmail. We've talked about this. We have to wait and see what he'll do, how he'll play his hand. He might not even mention it."

Ben snorted. Yeah, right. He won't say anything. Ben knew he would. He knew! He'd been with Edward enough times to know the kind of man he was. If he could use this knowledge to his advantage, then he would. He wanted Geoff's business, and this was the perfect way to get it.

Why Edward wanted Ben, he didn't know. He could pay for anyone on the streets, shit, why he did though was beyond Ben. Maybe it was the element of being able to control them, but wasn't there a place he could go for that?

"Geoff?"

"Yeah."

"Why the streets? I mean, Edward likes being in control, so why not some of the places you know? Or escorts?"

Ben watched Geoff lean back in his chair, a thoughtful expression on his face.

"He wouldn't be able to use escorts. He would have to register, and if he went beyond the limits the agency had, then they would remove him from their books. As for clubs, well we've already discussed why

New Beginnings

he wouldn't last there, so that would leave the streets."

"Do you miss it? The club?" Geoff had told him he hadn't been recently.

"I miss certain aspects. I miss the friends I've made there. It's not all about the BDSM. You're part of a group, with people who like the same things you do. Some people hear about this lifestyle and immediately think you're a deviant, a sadist. It's not like that. It's a community, a community with people who share the same interests as you and know they won't be judged for it. The people who go are from all walks of life, so obviously there is a lot of discretion involved. Safety is paramount, hence contracts, safe words, a full monitoring system, background checks, et cetera."

"I know. I see the way you take care of me. You always make sure that I'm okay with what we're doing."

"I was worried. I wasn't sure you would want anything to do with me when I told you. You've been through so much already, and then to tell you what I like sexually?" Geoff shook his head. "I thought I'd pushed you away."

"No. I like being able to give up control to you." Ben ducked his head, heat flooding his face. He did like it when Geoff was in control. After everything he'd experienced in his life, the constant need for control, it was freeing to be able to hand that over to someone else. Someone he trusted. Someone he was in love with.

"Don't be embarrassed. I love that I can do this for you. I..." Geoff suddenly looked away. Ben watched as Geoff stood up and took his plate to the sink.

"I what?" Ben asked him. He was sure Geoff had been about to say something more, so why had he stopped?

"Nothing," Geoff smiled at him.

Ben froze, his chest tightening painfully. "No, please tell me," Ben begged him.

Geoff turned, rubbing his hands over his face. Oh god. It was something he'd done. Ben felt sick. He knew this would happen, knew that he would do something wrong and end up back on the streets. Who had he been kidding? He was a fuck up, and he deserved this.

"I love you, Ben."

Ben frowned, shaking his head, "Sorry?" What had he just said? Did he just say that?

"I love you. I know it's probably too soon, and God knows I'm too old for you, but yes, there it is."

"You love me?" Ben struggled to wrap his head around it. Geoff loved *him*?

Geoff nodded, looking at Ben with his head tilted to the side, as if he was studying him. Ben's chest tightened and he swallowed past the lump in his throat. Only his Nan had ever said she'd loved him. He'd always thought that no one would be able to love him, especially when they found out that he'd sold himself. He took a deep, shuddering breath. He could feel his eyes itching as they filled with tears, and he couldn't stop them from falling.

"Hey, there's no need to cry. I shouldn't have said anything. I didn't mean to upset you."

Ben shook his head as Geoff wrapped him in his arms, holding him tight. He hugged Geoff to him. "I didn't think anyone would love me," he told him as he hiccupped before another wave of tears started. "I didn't think anyone would see me." He struggled to speak past the lump in his throat.

"Oh, Ben. You are so worth loving. Well, maybe not when you first came here."

Ben coughed out a laugh. Yeah, he hadn't been nice when he came here. He'd isolated himself, threw things and shouted. Geoff lifted his head up, looking into his eyes.

"I love you, Ben," he told him again.

Ben tried a weak smile as he sniffed. Wow, that sounded nice. Geoff passed him some tissues, and he blew his nose, wiping his eyes. He took a shaky breath in and released it. At least he wasn't alone with these feelings.

"I love you too."

"You don't have to say it back."

"No! That's not why I'm saying it! I've... I've had these feelings for a while now, but I was too afraid to say anything. I didn't want to lose you. Every time I thought about telling you, I was afraid you'd ask me to leave. All I could think about was how you'd react. I mean, a whore telling you he loved you."

"Stop thinking of yourself like that. You are more than that, you know this. That was what you did. It's not who you are. I've never told anyone I loved them, well, except my family, so this is new for me too."

"Yeah?"

"Yes." Geoff smiled at him holding him at arm's length. "Let's tidy up and go upstairs."

Ben smirked at him. "You want some sex?" he asked jokingly.

"Well, we have just declared our love, so I think it's fitting, don't you?"

"I got my results back and I'm clean, so we don't have to use anything. Can you..." He wanted to be tied up again. He loved it when Geoff tied him up and took control.

"What? All you have to do is ask."

"Cuffs..." God, why was it so difficult to ask him this?

"You want me to cuff you?"

Ben could feel himself harden at the thought of Geoff cuffing him to the bed. He nodded, watching the change come over Geoff. It was the way he held himself that little bit straighter, a little bit taller, shoulders back.

"Go upstairs. Shower. Wait for me there. Oh, and Ben? I'm clean too."

Ben's breath caught in his chest and he got up and jogged upstairs. No condoms. What would it feel like to have Geoff inside him with nothing between them? He entered the bedroom and stripped off quickly before walking into the bathroom. He turned it on and waited for the temperature to adjust. He got in and turned his face up towards the spray, letting it wash the tears away. He felt a cold draft behind him and turned to see a naked Geoff sliding the door closed. Geoff swung the cuffs on his fingers, winking at him.

"Safe words."

"Dark for stop and grey to slow down, Sir."

"Good. Come when you want. Now, no talking."

"Yes, Sir."

Geoff fastened one of the cuffs to Ben's wrist then pulled his arm up above his head and passed it through a small grab rail before fastening it to his other wrist. Funny, Ben had never noticed the rail up there before. He tugged on the cuffs and heard the metal on metal sound as they clicked together.

Geoff knelt before him and slowly licked up his shaft, twirling his tongue around the head. Ben leaned his head back against the shower tiles, moaning. God, that felt good. Damn good. He groaned when Geoff sucked one of his balls into his mouth, running his tongue over the creased flesh. Geoff moved to the other one, licking over and around it. Ben spread his legs wide to give Geoff more space to kneel when Geoff grabbed his hips and spun him around so Ben was now facing the wall.

When Ben felt Geoff's tongue on his hole, he gasped, and then groaned. The sensation of his tongue licking and sucking him caused Ben to shiver in pleasure. Geoff could do wicked things with his tongue: licking around the wrinkled flesh with the tip of his tongue then using the flat of it to lick up and down his hole. The things Geoff could do with his mouth and tongue.

When Geoff's tongue speared his hole, Ben cried out, the cuffs rattling above him as his body jerked. Geoff fucked his arse with his tongue, his hands holding Ben's arse cheeks wide apart. Ben arched up, standing on tiptoe as Geoff's tongue flicked over his hole before sinking in again.

Losing track of time, Ben moaned loudly when two of Geoff's fingers speared inside. Spinning him back around, Geoff continued to push his fingers in and out of Ben as he sucked the head of his dick back into his mouth.

Ben couldn't stop jerking and shuddering, crying out as Geoff sucked him off and fucked him with his fingers, constantly rubbing on his hot spot. He could hear the cuffs above him as he moved his arms. He couldn't stop moving, his body a quaking mess as pleasure radiated through him. The dual sensations were too much for him to take.

Feeling a tingle start at the base of his spine, Ben's balls pulled up and he knew he was going to come.

"I'm coming, Sir!" Ben shouted out.

Within seconds, he was crying out, shooting into Geoff's mouth.

Every pulse of come tightened his muscle around Geoff's fingers that were still rubbing his prostate, prolonging his orgasm, keeping his body taut with pleasure.

Eventually his body sagged, all energy leaving it, and he slumped back on the tiled wall. Eyes squeezed tightly shut, mouth open and panting for breath, Ben wasn't aware Geoff had moved until he felt himself being lifted up. Ben automatically wrapped his legs around Geoff's waist and felt Geoff push in slowly past his muscle. Geoff adjusted his hold on him before allowing Ben to lower onto his cock. Ben could feel the fullness all the way in his chest and closed his eyes again as Geoff began to lift and lower him as he slowly fucked him against the shower wall. He could feel everything, the sensations so much sharper with nothing in between them.

It turned him on so much knowing that Geoff was strong enough to lift and hold him as he fucked him against the wall. He opened his eyes, looking into Geoff's. Geoff's pupils were blown wide with lust. It was a beautiful sight.

"I love you," Geoff whispered to him before licking across Ben's lips.

Ben opened his mouth and sucked Geoff's tongue in as Geoff sped up, hitting his sensitive spot with every thrust. Harder and faster, Geoff fucked him and Ben loved it. Loved the way Geoff held him. Loved the way Geoff ravaged his mouth. Loved the way he controlled his body. Loved the way he could just let go and fly. Fuck, Ben simply loved him.

Geoff was grunting with every thrust and Ben felt himself getting ready to come again, his dick hardening against his abs, but Ben wanted to come at the same time as Geoff. Geoff suddenly grabbed his thighs tightly and shuddered, crying out as he came and that triggered Ben's own orgasm.

Ben's balls tightened, and arcs of electricity raced through his body, his orgasm flooding over him. Ben came feeling the ropes splash up onto his chest and Ben moaned loudly, his dick twitching with every pump of come that left his slit.

How long they rested together, Ben didn't know, but he let Geoff take his weight as they both calmed down. Eventually, Geoff gently lowered him to his feet, pulling out. Ben's hole twitched and he felt Geoff's come leak from his arse, running down his thighs. Stood still, he watched Geoff clean him up, wiping his chest and abdomen before he turned him to clean his arse and thighs.

Ben winced. It was fantastic with nothing between them, all sensations magnified, but there was definitely more clean up involved.

When Ben was released from the cuffs, Geoff massaged his shoulders and arms, helping the blood flow return to them, then turned the shower off. Ben stood watching Geoff dry him then he took Ben's hand and pulled him towards the bed.

Ben crawled into the bed and moved over, leaving space for Geoff to crawl in behind him. He cuddled close, his head on Geoff's chest and closed his eyes. He felt so peaceful as he lay listening to Geoff's steady heartbeat.

He had always thought that he wasn't worthy of being loved. The way his parents had treated him, the abuse he had suffered at their hands, then having to sell himself on the streets to survive, had always made him think that this was what he deserved. To know that someone loved him and wanted him in their life was overwhelming, hence the tears, which he could have done without.

He hugged Geoff closer to him and felt him squeeze him back. "Are you alright?" Geoff asked him.

"Yeah, I am. I'm just....I don't know how to explain it."

"Too much, too soon?"

"No! God, no. I'm happy, really happy, Geoff. I just never expected any of it. After everything..." Ben began to choke up again as emotions overwhelmed him.

"Don't cry, Ben. I shouldn't have said anything."

"No, I'm glad you told me because that means I'm not on my own in these feelings. I've never thought I'd be lucky enough, that I deserved to be loved. I love you so much. I didn't know what it was I was feeling, but I knew that I didn't want to leave you."

"I don't want you to leave either. I love having you here." Geoff lifted Ben's head up off his chest. "I love you, don't forget that."

Ben nodded wiping his eyes. He couldn't believe he was crying again. Hadn't he done enough of that already?

"Get some sleep, Ben." Geoff leaned down kissing him softly on the lips.

"Night, Geoff."

"Night."

New Beginnings

Chapter Twenty

Monday came too soon, and Geoff was concerned as to what would happen in the meeting with Edward. He hoped Edward wouldn't make any threats, but knowing what the man was like, and his reputation as a shark, Geoff wouldn't be surprised if Edward did.

The rumours that Geoff had heard indicated that Edward wasn't always above board in his actions in gaining whatever business or client he wanted. Now that Edward knew about Ben, he had enough information to act on and try to force Geoff into either a merger or force him to sell the business.

Geoff walked into his office and sat down behind his desk. He wasn't surprised when Seb poked his head in a few minutes later. "Today's the day, right?"

"Yes. He should be here for ten."

"How have you and Ben been?" Seb asked, walking into the office and sitting down.

"Ben's worried, but that's no surprise. As for me... Well, I just want to know how he's going to play his cards. He knows about Ben, and it's just what he'll do with that knowledge."

"He wants in here. Any way he can," Seb muttered, frowning.

"Absolutely. He's been trying for a couple of years now. We're not interested. He doesn't have a good reputation, and we don't want to be associated with him."

"I'm going to go back to my desk, but do you want me in here when he comes?" Seb asked as he stood.

"No. We'll stick to the plan. I've got the detective's number, and I'll call her after the meeting." Geoff shrugged. "He might not say anything."

Seb snorted. "Yeah, right."

Geoff smiled at him. "I'm trying to remain positive that he only has good intentions."

They looked at each other for a few seconds before they both chuckled.

"Yeah, good luck with that," Seb told him as he walked out of Geoff's office.

Geoff worked until he heard the receptionist tell him that Edward was waiting. Geoff walked to the reception area and found Edward sat waiting. Showtime.

"Morning, Edward. Come through to my office and we'll get started. Do you want something to drink?"

"Coffee will be fine, thank you." Edward smiled.

As they walked into Geoff's office, he paused and asked Sue, his receptionist, to get them some coffee. He didn't usually ask her to do this, but with the situation as it was, he didn't want to leave Edward alone in his office.

"Edward, please sit. The coffee will be here soon. Now, what can I help you with?"

Edward smiled at him as he sat, and Geoff couldn't help but think of how slimy he looked at that moment. He had a nasty gleam to his eyes, and Geoff knew that Edward would use whatever he could to get what he wanted.

They waited until the coffee was served, then Edward said, "You know I've been interested in a merger between our businesses."

"Yes, and the answer is the same. I'm flattered, but no, we're not interested at this time."

He watched Edward lean back in his chair, putting the ankle of one foot on the knee of the other. He gave him a slick smile.

"I thought that might be the answer," Edward paused, taking a sip of his coffee. "That function the other night was quite the eye opener, wasn't it?"

"No more so than usual," Geoff knew exactly where Edward was going with this and carefully kept his face blank.

"That boy you had with you. What was his name again?"

"Ben, and he isn't a boy."

"Oh no, no, he isn't, is he?" Edward commented in a tone that sounded calculated to Geoff.

Geoff frowned at Edward. He would go along with this and see where he went with it.

"Is that supposed to mean something?"

"What?" Edward smiled at him again. "How long have you known Ben for?"

"I'm sorry. I thought we were here to discuss a possible merger, not the person I brought to The Lowry."

"Oh, I'm sorry. I didn't realise it was a touchy subject," Edward said in a syrupy voice.

"So, the answer is still the same, Edward. At this moment in time, we aren't interested in a merger with your company." Geoff smiled politely at him. He wanted him out of his office, but knew he had to wait and bide his time. Edward was going somewhere with this.

"Ben. He's a nice looking young man, isn't he? Where did you meet him?"

"Is this relevant, Edward?" He was going to make Edward work for it.

"Just making conversation. I'm curious. I know someone who also knows Ben. You're aware of his past employment, aren't you?"

Geoff coughed. Past employment? That was a delicate way of putting it. "Yes, I am. Why?"

"It doesn't concern you, what he does?"

"What he did, and no, it doesn't. Why should it?"

"You wouldn't want it to become common knowledge now, would you? Being associated with a known prostitute? How would that affect you and your business? If your clients found out, do you think they would stay?"

"How would they find out, Edward? Only you and I know what Ben used to do. Who is this person that knows about Ben? Someone who used to go to him, perhaps? Someone who used to pay him for his services?"

Edward shrugged, sipping his coffee, seemingly calm and collected. "That's not really any concern of mine. Just think about what

I said. You don't want anyone to know about your relationship with Ben."

"What would your advice be, Edward?"

"Well, I wouldn't stay with Ben. I hope it isn't serious?" Edward seemed to look genuinely concerned. Geoff was actually amazed at how well Edward was performing. The man was that good; he should have gone into acting.

Geoff shrugged. "Well, I'm not sure what it is."

"That's good. You know I want in with your business, so think about my proposal. Oh, and stop seeing Ben. You wouldn't want people to find out about your association with him, would you?" Edward smoothed his tie as he stood. Bending down to pick his suitcase up, Edward added, "I'm sure you'll find that the terms and conditions of the merger are quite favourable for you. I'll speak to you soon, Geoff. Think about what I've said."

Geoff watched Edward walk out of his office before slumping back in his chair. It was how he had expected it to be. Nothing was said outright, but he had hinted at it. Oh, he had hinted at it. Drop Ben and sign a merger or people would find out about Ben and his past. He knew it could affect his business if it became common knowledge, let alone the damage it would do to Ben, and he was finally moving on from his past. His sessions with Clara were obviously helping him, and this would set him back.

Geoff sighed, thinking over his next steps. He had no choice but to inform the police about this. It was all insinuation though; nothing outright had been said. He took the card with the detective's details out of his drawer and stared at it before finally calling the number.

The detective answered on the fourth ring.

"Hello, Detective Jacobs speaking."

"Hi, it's Geoff Foster here. I was wondering if I could talk to you for a minute."

"Sure. How can I help you?"

"It's not related to Adam's murder. It's about a meeting I've just finished here."

"Go on." The detective sounded intrigued.

"As you know, Ben Parker lives with me, and he attended a function that was held at The Lowry and we ran into one of his ex-customers. Unfortunately, this ex-customer recognised Ben."

"Did he comment on it?"

"He's wanted to merge with my company for a couple of years now, and I've always said no. Today, we had a meeting, and he insinuated how it would be bad for business if clients found about Ben. He suggested I have nothing to do with him, and he left a copy of his terms for the merger."

There was silence on the line, then the detective spoke. "Subtle, very subtle. As you've said, he's insinuated but not made any direct demands."

"He wants another meeting and I'm fairly certain if I refuse to meet him or refuse to meet his demands, then it won't be long before rumours start."

"Is he aware that you know he paid for Ben's services?" Jacobs asked.

"No. I made sure not to say anything, and it was a friend who knew Ben, not Edward."

"Of course it was. The classic friend line. How can I help you?"

"I wanted to record the next meeting. It's blackmail regardless of how he does it."

"I agree, but as you said, he hasn't said anything outright."

"So, what can I do? He's a solicitor, so he knows how to play this situation."

The detective sighed, then asked, "What's his name?"

"Edward Chambers."

"Edward Chambers? As in Edward Chambers of Chambers and Chambers?"

"Yes. Why?" Geoff asked her, puzzled by her response when he named Edward.

"I'm sorry, but I can't tell you that. When is this meeting?"

"Nothing has been arranged yet. I'm expecting a call Monday or Tuesday."

"Call me when you know and we'll be there."

"Okay, thanks."

"I don't need to tell you that the fewer people who know about this, the better."

"Yes, I understand."

"Oh, and have Mr Foster come in and make a statement as to what's happened between them. That will help any case we might have."

"I'll speak to him now."

"Goodbye, and thanks for the call."

"You're welcome."

Geoff hung up and thought about the conversation he'd just had. It sounded like they knew something about Edward and his business dealings. So, those rumours could hold some truth to them. It had always surprised him when certain long-standing and supposedly reputable companies had sold to Chambers and Chambers.

Sighing, he picked up the phone and spoke to Seb, asking him to come to his office. A couple of minutes later, Seb was sat in front of him, patiently waiting for Geoff to speak.

"I need Tom to go with Ben to the police station to make a statement."

"So, it's on."

"The fewer details people know, the better the outcome."

"No, I understand. I'll go tell Tom and ask him to go after work." Seb started to stand when he saw Geoff shaking his head.

"No. I would like it to be done now. I'll call Ben and let him know."

"Alright. I'll tell Tom now." As Seb walked towards the door, Geoff spoke.

"Thanks for this, Seb."

Seb held the door open with his hand and faced Geoff. "Everyone deserves a second chance, don't they? Why should Ben have to have his past held over him, forced to do something he doesn't want to. He wants to be with you, but we both know that he doesn't want his past to affect you either. Not so long ago, he would have just walked, but now? Now he wants to stay, and that's down to you."

Seb closed the door behind him after he finished speaking, and Geoff stared at it for a long time going over what Seb had just said. Seb was right. Ben would have been long gone weeks ago if this situation had occurred then. Geoff reached over and picked up the phone, calling Ben. He answered on the second ring.

"Well?"

Geoff chuckled quietly. "'Hi Geoff. How did the meeting go?'

Well, Ben. It went as we thought it would do, but don't worry, I've spoken to the detective and everything will be alright."

"Okay, sorry, but I've been sat here shitting myself, thinking all sorts of stuff. Wondering what the fuck was going on?"

"It's alright, Ben. Really it is. Tom's on his way over and you're going the station to make a statement. The detective will be waiting for you."

"So, they're on board then?"

"Looks that way. Will you be alright? I know this isn't going to be easy for you."

"No, it's not." Ben laughed humourlessly. "But, it needs to be done." Geoff heard him exhale heavily. "I'll have Tom with me."

"Want me to come as well?"

"No, but thanks anyway. Do your thing and I'll see you tonight. It's lamb for dinner."

"My favourite."

Ben laughed again. "I'll let you know how it goes when you get home tonight. Love you."

"Love you too."

Geoff dropped the phone on the desk, stood and walked over to the window. He stood staring out at the people below as they hurried about. Tom would be on his way over to Ben now, even though Ben had told him he didn't need him to accompany him. A huge part of Geoff wanted to be there with him. Ben had made great progress since he had tried to kill himself, their sex life being one of them, but issues like this might set him back. Having to go to the police and discuss what it was you had to do to survive, especially with someone like Edward, must be appalling for him.

Geoff sighed, walking back to his desk and sitting down on the chair. Why couldn't life be simple? Two men meet and fall in love, but life didn't always happen like that. Life was full of ups and downs and bumps in the road. He was lucky he had such a supportive family and good friends to help him through those difficult times. Shaking his head, Geoff brought up his itinerary for the rest of the day and began to go through his work.

New Beginnings

Chapter Twenty-One

To say the experience at the police station had been humiliating and degrading would have been a massive understatement. The detective had been wonderful though and had tried her best to put Ben at ease, but the questions she had asked? And having to go through his time with Edward and tell a stranger what he'd allowed Edward to do to him. It had left a sour taste in his mouth and he'd squirmed on the hard chair as he'd gone through the details. Ben had never been so happy to leave a place as he was when he was finally able to walk out. Fortunately, Tom had stayed with him the entire time, and the woman had even allowed him to come into the interview, which he thought they wouldn't have.

As soon as Ben had walked through the front door, he'd taken a long, hot shower to try and wash the dirt away. He'd dressed in clean clothes then started preparing dinner in an attempt to forget about his visit to the police station. As the meat was cooking, he sat at the table and wrote in his journal. The writing had turned out to be a cathartic experience for him and he'd been surprised at what he had written. The memories he'd suppressed came rushing back to the surface and he was able to write them down. When he read them again, he found they didn't hold quite the same power over him that they once had.

He checked the time and went to put the finishing touches to the meal. Geoff arrived home then, and immediately went over to him, pulling him into a tight hug.

"Are you alright?"

Ben nodded into his chest. "Yeah. I knew it would be difficult, so I'm glad Tom was there with me. Thanks for sending him." Ben looked up into Geoff's eyes.

"He wanted to be there with you. Did it go well?"

"Yeah. She was nice, surprisingly. She didn't seem to judge me. Normally, the cops look at you like scum, but not her."

"The few dealings I've had with her, she always comes across as genuine."

"She said my statement will help. When will you meet him again?" Ben asked him. He wanted to know when all this would finally be over. Just when he thought he was finally getting his life back on track, Edward came worming his way into it.

"I'm expecting a call Monday or Tuesday. With a meeting to be arranged. Everything's set up with the police so we'll just have to wait and see." Walking over to the oven, Geoff peered inside. "That lamb smells wonderful. How long?"

"Enough time for you to freshen up. Go and get ready. I'll start serving when you come back down."

Geoff kissed him before leaving the kitchen and Ben smiled to himself as he started to serve the veg he'd cooked to go with the lamb. A few minutes later, Geoff came back into the kitchen and took a couple of bottle of beers from the fridge.

"Beer with lamb?" Ben questioned him.

Geoff shrugged. "Feel like a beer tonight."

Ben shook his head as he finished serving up the food. They sat down to eat, and there was silence for a good ten minutes as they ate.

Geoff leaned back when he had finished and patted his full stomach. "That was great, Ben!"

"Thanks. The beer went well too." Ben smirked at him.

"Hey. I can do a beer every now and again, and after Edward, I needed one." Geoff frowned as he talked.

Ben stood and started to clear the dishes. After loading up the dishwasher, he walked into the living room to find Geoff rummaging through the DVDs there. He held a couple up for him before asking, "Fancy one?"

Ben had a quick look. "Indiana Jones?"

"My choice too. Grab us another couple of beers and I'll set it up."

Within a few minutes, they were both sat on the sofa, Geoff's arm around Ben's shoulders, as the film started. Ben rested his head on Geoff's chest and felt like he could truly relax for the first time that day.

※ ※ ※

The week went quickly, but Edward didn't call to arrange another meeting. Ben wasn't sure why, unless he was delaying contacting Geoff on purpose, to cause anxiety. On Saturday, they went out into the city centre and browsed the shops before having a heavenly Italian meal at this little restaurant that Geoff frequented. On Sunday, they went out with Tom and Seb for a few hours then popped back to their house and had dinner there with Matt and Luke. It was nice to catch up with everyone again. It had seemed such a long time ago that all four of them had sat in the same room as each other when they had discussed Adam's funeral. Ben liked the fact that they were all starting to get on with their lives.

Matt and Luke would be doing their A-Levels with him, and Tom was going to do his GCSEs. Tom had told Ben that he wanted to do the same job as Seb, so he knew he had a lot of studying ahead of him, but he seemed happy; in fact, they all did. It was hard to think that this time the year before they had been struggling to survive. Doing whatever they had to just to be able to afford to eat and drink, living in an abandoned house that was cold and damp. When they finally left and got home, Ben was exhausted and fell into a deep sleep as soon as his head hit the pillow.

Monday found him sat in the kitchen, unable to concentrate on anything. Would Edward call today? Would he arrange a meeting with Geoff? What about the police? Would they get involved? There had been no calls over the weekend, well, none that he knew about, so what would happen? He sat on the stool, leg bouncing as he tried to do some research on the courses he planned on taking at college. He'd always loved science, learning how things were made or how they evolved, how certain chemicals came together or how something invisible like gravity could affect so much around it. He'd never felt a leaning towards one type of science but had loved all science.

The phone rang, startling him and he hurried over to it. "Hello."

"It's me, Ben." Geoff answered him.

"Has he been in touch?" Ben asked, his stomach tied up in knots.

"Yes. Meeting is scheduled for Wednesday. Police know and will be here recording it."

"So they want to be involved?"

"Appears that way. Seems they've been after Edward for some time, but have never been able to get anything solid on him."

"You'll have to get him to talk then."

"Yeah." Ben heard Geoff sigh over the phone. "Not sure how yet, other than to just keep refusing, try and call his bluff."

"When I had... when I was with him..." Ben paused. How could he talk about his times with Edward?

"It's alright, Ben. Say what you need to."

Ben inhaled deeply then blew out. "Edward likes to be in charge. If I didn't do what he wanted when he wanted it, I was punished. He would hurt me. He liked it, inflicting pain, and he would remind me who was in charge, who had control over my body. Not like when I'm with you, though. You make me feel like the most important person in the room." Ben took a deep breath in then released it. "So, what I'm trying to say is I would think if he felt like he wasn't in control of the situation you might see his true colours."

"Take away his perceived control." Silence from Geoff, then he said, "Yeah, I can work with that. You're right, he likes to dictate. In pretty much every meeting I've seen him in, he likes to take control of it. Turn the meeting in the direction he wanted it to go in. So, I need to set the tone as soon as he walks in that I'm in charge, and nothing he has to say will change that."

Ben nodded to himself. "Yeah. It'll frustrate him that he can't get what he wants and that in turn will anger him. He obviously believes that because he knows me and what I used to do, he can use that to his advantage. He probably thinks I haven't told you about him, but really, who in their right mind would think that?"

"He could think that you would be too ashamed to mention it. Who knows? Look, I've got to get going but I wanted you to know, alright? I'll see you at home. Oh, and Ben? You are the most important person to me. Don't ever forget that."

Ben stood by the counter staring absently at the phone he'd put down. Wednesday was the day he would finally be able to be free of his past, finally be able to move on with his life. It had taken such a long time to get here, though he was honest enough to admit he hadn't helped himself, and he felt like he was finally able to breathe again.

Geoff.

Ben wouldn't be where he was today if it weren't for Geoff. God, he'd hated the man at first. Ben chuckled to himself. But Geoff had turned out to be the one person who wanted to be with him, regardless of his past. The sex was amazing and after everything he had been forced to do, sex had been the last thing on his mind, yet with Geoff, he was discovering parts of himself he never knew existed. Who knew he liked to be dominated in bed? The fact that Geoff always made sure he had as much pleasure as possible, that he always made sure he was taken care of, was amazing. He'd never had any of that when he was on the streets. It was always a quick fuck or more often, a blow job. He only had sex if he was really desperate for money. Adam and Tom had taught him that.

He sighed, gently shaking his head. Now wasn't the time to think about it. That was the past, and even though he could never change it, he certainly could move on from it. His sessions with Clara had shown him that. The way Geoff treated him showed him that. He took a deep breath and held it for a minute before releasing it and smiling. It would all be over soon.

※ ※ ※

New Beginnings

Wednesday came around too soon, and Geoff sat in his office waiting for Edward to arrive. The meeting had been arranged for nine, and the police had already been in and set up all their equipment and now Geoff was sat at his desk waiting. Though he was a patient man and usually found these quiet times relaxing, he felt restless and uneasy, his body jittery. He found he couldn't settle and had to constantly move, doing anything to distract himself from what was happening. He wanted this to be over and done with.

Geoff's secretary buzzed him, alerting him to Edward's arrival. He wiped his hands on his pants, realising that he was sweating and walked to his office door, opening it. He smiled at Sue and then extended his hand to Edward.

"Good Morning, Edward. Please come in." He turned to Sue. "Could you get us some coffee, please?"

Sue rolled her eyes at him. "Of course." She winked at him as she stood and walked towards the small break area.

Geoff closed the door behind him and sat behind his desk. He looked up at Edward and smiled. "How was your weekend, Edward? Did you have a nice time with your family?"

"Yes, yes. Now, have you had a chance to look at the details I left on Friday?"

So, straight down to business. "Yes, I have, thanks. Again, I'm sorry, but at this time we aren't currently looking for a merger or to sell the business."

Geoff noticed Edward frown slightly.

"Really? I thought the details were quite favourable for you."

"Yes, they were, but we're happy as we are." Geoff heard the knock on the door as Sue entered with their coffees. "Thank you, Sue."

Sue stood behind Edward's back and stuck her tongue out at him.

Geoff looked at her with a raised brow, but she merely shrugged and closed the door behind her.

"How was Ben when you ended things with him?"

"Oh, we haven't ended things."

"Really? Him being a prostitute doesn't concern you?"

"He *was* a prostitute, Edward. He isn't one now."

Edward smiled slightly, reaching for his coffee, and took a sip. Geoff needed him to say something, anything to incriminate himself. He wanted Ben to be free from him.

"It doesn't concern you that if your clients found out about him, it may impact your business? You're willing to lose potential customers?"

Geoff spread his arms wide. "How would they find out, Edward? Only you and I know about his past, and we wouldn't tell anyone, would we?" Come on, take the bait!

Edward sighed dramatically, seeming to look genuinely sorry as he spoke. "Well, I couldn't keep something like that a secret. People have a right to know the type of man they would be employing, don't you think? How would it look? The man they were trusting to win their case was consorting with a known prostitute and God knows what else. I can't imagine he relied on prostitution alone to survive, can you? I wonder what other criminal acts he perpetrated. You really can't afford that type of information to get out can you?"

"So, you think I should finish things with him and then what? What will become of him?"

Edward gave him a smile that didn't reach his eyes. "Oh, someone as good looking as him will no doubt find someone to take care of him. You know it's best for you to end things, don't you?"

"No. I don't think I want to end things with him. I'm happy with him, and his past doesn't bother me."

"Well, you leave me no choice then, Geoff." Edward sat back in his chair and folded his hands together looking at Geoff contemplatively.

"No choice?" Geoff played dumb.

"I'll have to let my business partners know about Ben. It's a shame really, I like you, Geoff. I was hoping we could work together in the future."

"Let me get this straight. If I stay with Ben, you'll tell people about our relationship."

"Like I said, you leave me no choice. Potential clients deserve to know the truth. A known prostitute and possibly a thief. That knowledge could affect your credibility."

"So if I finish with Ben, you'll stay quiet."

Edward smiled again. "Let's talk about the merger, shall we."

"There will be no merger, Edward."

"Oh, I think there will be. Ben, remember?"

"Hang on. Let me get this straight. If I don't finish with Ben and sign the papers for the merger, you'll tell people about us? Really? Do you seriously think that people knowing about my relationship with Ben would have that much of an impact on my business?"

"I do. Chinese whispers. One innocent comment in the right ear can cause serious problems for your business. We both know that. I want your business, and I have no problem doing what I have to, to get it. I will ruin you. Maybe I should, it would probably cost me less to buy you outright when you're ruined, then I'll own your company."

Geoff stared at Edward. Wow, he really was something. He knew he wanted Edward to threaten his business, but witnessing him in action was something else. He did all with a smile on his face!

"Look, there's no need for this."

"I think there is, Geoff. I want your company, and I want you to get rid of Ben, and I have the information that can damage you, which I will use if I have to. Sign the forms and save yourself a lot of heartache and misery. I don't want to ruin your reputation, but if you leave me no choice, I will destroy you. Imagine what people will think? Your boyfriend's a prostitute. How many did you use before you found the right one? How much money did you spend fucking your way through them all? Using and abusing them. Whispers, Geoff, can cause so much damage."

Geoff raised his eyebrows at Edward. "I can't believe you'd go to this extent just to get me to sign a contract with you. Why? There are plenty of other businesses out there for you. Why mine?"

"Your father was a wonderful man and he has built up an impressive company with a fabulous reputation, which you have carried on. My name merged with that?" Edward smiled again.

"The answer's no. I won't sign anything, and Ben stays with me."

Geoff watched Edward clench his jaw, gripping his hands tightly together. He leaned forward, staring into Geoff's eyes.

"You really don't want to mess with me, Geoff. I can ruin you. Is that what you want? When I'm finished with you, there will be nothing left to salvage. You and your business will be destroyed. I've done it before, and I can do it again. I always get what I want." Edward paused, giving Geoff a slight smile. "Remember Thomas Standing? He said no to me, and where is he now? Hmm. Not working, is he? His business is finished. He said no to me, and I ruined him. It was easier than I thought it would be. The right comments said in the right ears, and it spreads like wildfire, and before you know it, boom, the business is gone. I'll do the same to you, Geoff. I want your business, so sign."

Geoff was stunned, staring at Edward with his mouth falling open. Had he ruined Thomas? Surely this was enough for the police. Where the fuck were they? Why hadn't they come charging in and arrested him? What else could they need?

"So you caused Thomas' business to end. Who else, Edward? Who else have you destroyed? Who else have you blackmailed? Who else has lost their livelihood because you wouldn't take no for an answer?"

Edward smiled sickly sweet at him. "Now, now. I'm not going to tell you every conquest, am I? And I don't call it blackmail. All I have to do is say a word or two in the right ears and..." Edward face suddenly transformed, and he stared at Geoff maliciously. "Sign, Geoff. Don't give me a reason to ruin you too. Once you've signed, we can talk about how to end things with Ben."

"No."

Edward shook his head, leaning forward in his chair. "You leave me no choice then. Good luck, Geoff, you're going to need it. When I've finished with you, you'll have nothing. No business, your reputation ruined, and no..."

It was at that moment the door flew open, and the room filled with officers. Edward was handcuffed and led from the room, smiling as he went. Geoff sat back wearily in his chair, closing his eyes and rubbing his forehead.

He heard someone clearing their throat and opened his eyes to the male detective who had turned up that morning.

"Was it enough?" he asked him.

"You were fantastic. Really. We had always wondered about Thomas Standing, but there was hardly any information to incriminate Edward. Are you up to answering a few questions?"

Geoff nodded as he pinched the bridge of his nose. He just wanted this to be finally over.

Chapter Twenty-Two

By the time Geoff got home, Ben was frantic. Geoff hadn't called him once today to let him know what had happened in his meeting with Edward. Had Edward threatened him? Had the police gotten the information they needed? Had Edward been arrested? On and on, the thoughts scrambled around in his head and he was slowly going out of this mind when he heard the key in the door.

Ben rushed to the door and was going to demand Geoff answer his questions when he saw his face. Geoff looked pale and drawn. He looked exhausted with dark circles under his eyes. What the fuck had happened?

"Sit down and I'll get you as a drink."

Ben rushed into the living room and poured a shot of whisky for Geoff. He didn't think beer or wine would be good enough. He heard a noise in the doorway and saw Geoff standing there, staring at him intently. Oh, this didn't look good. Again, what the fuck happened?

"Is everything okay?"

Geoff nodded, walking over and taking the glass out of Ben's hand, pulling him in for a hug. He squeezed him so tightly that Ben thought he might die from lack of oxygen. Geoff suddenly released him, kissing him fiercely on the lips. Ben groaned, opening his mouth, taking Geoff's tongue in and stroking it with his own. They kissed like this for several minutes before Geoff eventually ended it and rested his forehead against Ben's.

"I love you, you know that, right?"

Ben nodded. Where had that come from? What had been said today?

"They've arrested him and they got it all on tape. Threatening to ruin my business and he admitted to doing the same to someone else's. I had to answer questions for hours afterwards. Go over everything. When I left, they informed me they were searching his home and businesses for further evidence. They had warrants in place and were just waiting to see how the meeting went. They said they have enough to prosecute him. It seems he wasn't content to just spread rumours. Apparently they have already found incriminating evidence at his home and work. They couldn't tell me a lot." Geoff shrugged.

"So it's over, right? No more threats, and we don't have to worry about him coming after your business again?" Ben asked him with trepidation and some small amount of hope to finally have this over and done with and to be able to live without this fear hanging over him.

"No more threats. We may have to go to court. It depends on his legal team and how he pleads, but yeah, it's over with."

Ben stepped back into Geoff's arms and dropped his head onto his chest. He breathed in deeply, taking in Geoff's unique scent, one he loved that reminded him of home. He suddenly felt like the weight of the world had been lifted from him, and he could finally breathe again.

"I love you, Geoff."

"I love you, too. Now, what's for dinner?"

Ben laughed, looking up at the man who had saved him and had given him a new life, a second chance. Taking his hand, he walked them out of the living room and into a new life filled with love and hope.

Epilogue

About a year later...

Ben smiled when arms wrapped around his waist and lips pressed a kiss to the back of his neck. Placing the wooden spoon in the pan, he raised his arm and threaded his fingers through Geoff's hair, pulling him closer.

"How did it go?"

Ben felt his breath on the back of his neck when Geoff sighed. "We won. I'm glad it's over and done with now."

"And Seb's case?"

"We lost."

"You both expected that to happen and at least Tom will be there for him." Ben reminded him.

Twisting in his arms, Ben faced him and wrapped his arms around Geoff's neck, tugging him down for a kiss. When they separated, Geoff said, "I know, but I hate to lose a case. Seb didn't do anything wrong. It was the outcome we both knew would happen."

"Lamb and veg for us and cheesy pasta for the boys, before you ask."

Geoff smiled, leaning down to kiss Ben again. "My favourite. You didn't have to go to all this trouble."

"I know, but I wanted to. You've worked so hard these last couple of weeks. Going in early and finishing late and by the time you've come home, you've been asleep before your head's hit the pillow."

New Beginnings

"Sorry, babe." Geoff kissed him again. Longer, deeper. Tongues tasting each other as they danced languidly.

Ben moaned. Even thought they'd been together for over a year, the sex between them remained off the chart. He couldn't get enough of Geoff, and he was the same way. The last two weeks had been hard, pun intended.

Breaking the kiss, Ben said, "Go. Shower. They'll be here soon."

"Love you." With one final kiss, Geoff left the kitchen and Ben watched him go.

So much had changed in the past year, the majority for the better. But, there were a couple of times when Ben had struggled. Adams funeral had been one of them. Watching his coffin move away as it went into the crematorium. That absolute concrete knowledge that Adam was dead. It had hit all of them hard, but thankfully, Seb and Geoff had been there for them.

The other one was the fallout from Edwards blackmailing scheme. With all the evidence the police had gathered, Edward had wisely pleaded guilty and had been sentenced to ten years in prison.

Ben sighed. All water under a bridge now, or so the saying went.

Thirty minutes later and the front door bell rang. Geoff went to open it, and Ben pulled out a chilled bottle of white wine from the fridge and poured three glasses. Lou was the DD for the night so for her, Charlie and Finley, Ben gave them orange juice.

As usual, Geoff came in with both boys attached to him, laughing as they tried to pull him over and start a wrestling match. Lou smiled as she shook her head. Ben hugged both Lou and Harry and passed them their drinks. No sooner had he handed them their glasses them he heard his name shouted.

"Uncle Ben!"

He turned and caught Finley as he threw himself into his arms. Ben lifted him up and, as he passed Geoff, took both Charlie and Finlay into the living room. After a couple of minutes, he heard a raised voices coming from the kitchen and walked in, seeing Geoff hugging Lou.

"Hey, is everything okay?" Ben asked as he slowly approached them.

Lou looked like she was crying but strangely smiling at the same time. She handed him a picture, and as Ben looked at it, he realised it was a scan. He furrowed his brow as he counted arms and legs.

"Er, did something go wrong? There's too many..."

"Twins," Harry said, grinning widely.

"Twins?" Ben repeated.

"Yes. My poor body. I won't be the size of a house. I'll be the size of a mansion!" Lou exclaimed. "Why did I let you talk me into it?"

"Because you love me and because you want a little girl." Harry reminded her.

"Knowing my luck, they'll be boys." Turning to face Ben, Lou asked, "So, how do you feel being the uncle to four little terrors?"

"I...wow. I just..."

"Our family is getting bigger, isn't it?" Geoff stood behind Ben and pulled him back to his chest.

Ben nodded, staring at the scan again. Was it only a year ago that he had been living on the streets with no family of his own? And now he was going to be the uncle of not two, but four children.

He looked at Harry and Lou then up at Geoff, swallowing past the sudden lump in his throat. "Our family," he muttered.

"Yes. Our family."

New Beginnings

He was home.

The End

About the Author

Megs Pritchard lives in England and is a mother to two small boys. When she isn't working or being mummy, she is busy writing about complex characters that know the harsh realities of life but want a HEA.

A lover of M/M and M/F romances she believes everyone deserves to be happy, healthy and loved.

Growing up in a military family, Megs has travelled Europe and has a great deal of respect and gratitude for all the men and women who have and who still serve. Her dream job was to be a Bomb Disposal Expert and even had her own 'kit' when she was younger.

She is currently working on her first full length series called Second Chances.

Coming Soon

The Bonds Within

Book Three in the Second Chances Series

Releasing 2017

Breaking Free

Book Four in the Second Chances Series

Releasing Dec 2017

Books by Megs Pritchard

Valentine's Surprise - Standalone Novella

Crossing Desires Series:
Awakening
Struggle

Terrible Twos - Standalone Novel

Second Chances Series:
Take a Chance

New Beginnings

Contact Information

You can learn more about Megs' writing at:

http://www.megspritchardauthor.com

Or you can follow her on:

Facebook: https://www.facebook.com/megspritchardauthor/

Instagram:https://www.instagram.com/megspritchardauthor/?hl=en

Twitter: https://twitter.com/megspritchard1

Tumble: https://www.tumblr.com/blog/megspritchard

Pinterest: https://uk.pinterest.com/megspritchard1/

Printed in Poland
by Amazon Fulfillment
Poland Sp. z o.o., Wrocław